TWILIGHT

AND OTHER STORIES

Other books in English
by Shulamith Hareven

City of Many Days
The Miracle Hater
Prophet

TWILIGHT

AND OTHER STORIES

SHULAMITH HAREVEN

Translated by Miriam Arad, Hillel Halkin,
J. M. Lask, and David Weber

Mercury House
San Francisco

Copyright © 1992 by Shulamith Hareven

Published in the United States by
Mercury House
San Francisco, California

Grateful acknowledgment is made to the original publishers of these stories in English: *The North American Review* for "The Emissary"; the Jewish Publication Society for "Twilight" (in *Facing the Holocaust: Selected Israeli Fiction*); Doubleday & Co. for "Loneliness" (in *Real Life*, a collection of stories by women writers from nine countries); *The Threepenny Review* for "My Straw Chairs"; and *Fiction Network* for "Love by Telephone."

United States Constitution, First Amendment: Congress shall make no law respecting an establishment of religion, or prohibiting the free exercise thereof; or abridging the freedom of speech, or of the press; or the right of the people peaceably to assemble, and to petition the Government for a redress of grievances.

Mercury House and colophon are registered trademarks
of Mercury House, Incorporated

Printed on acid-free paper
Manufactured in the United States of America

Library of Congress Cataloging-in-Publication Data

Hareven, Shulamith.
  Twilight and other stories / Shulamith Hareven.
     p.   cm.
  ISBN 1-56279-012-9
  1. Hareven, Shulamith—Translations into English. I. Title.
PJ5054.H292A2   1992
892.4'36—dc20   91-9959
                                                             CIP

*W*hen the Citie of Nola was over-run by the Barbarians, Paulinus Bishop thereof, having lost all he had there, and being their prisoner, prayed thus unto God: "Oh Lord deliver me from the feeling of this losse; for Thou knowest as yet they have touched nothing that is mine."

Montaigne, *Of Solitariness*

Contents

Twilight

*L*ast night I spent a year in the city where I was born. I had long known the password for getting there: Dante's line, "I am the way to the city of sorrow." In a clear voice I said: *"Per me si va nella città dolente,"* and time split open and I was there. In that one night's year I met a man, married, became pregnant, and gave birth to a murky child who grew fast, all without light.

*T*he city of my birth was very dark, extinguished, because the sun had left it and gone away a long, long time ago, and people in the street walked swiftly through the gloom, warming hands and lighting up faces with candles or matches. Here and there someone moved about with an oil lamp. The streets were wide, as I remembered them, but many windows were boarded up, the planks hammered in crosswise. Other windows were stuffed with rags and old newspapers against the cold. As there was no light, not a single tree was left in the streets, only black fenced-in staves. Not one plant showed on windowsills.

I saw no one I recognized at first, and yet everyone seemed very familiar, smiling faintly. They never went so far as to break into laughter. They already knew they would live without sun from now on, forever more. There was an air of humility and resignation about them. They were as kind to each other as they could be. Two acquaintances meeting in the street would warm one another's hands with a shy smile.

They wore the clothes I remembered from childhood: you could always tell a man's calling by his dress. Policemen wore a policeman's uniform, of course; the judge went about as a judge, alighting from his carriage in wig and gown; the chimney sweep was invariably in his work clothes, and so was the coachman, and so was the Count. The children were dressed as children: sailor collars and lace, and the girls with knees frozen in dresses of stiff scalloped taffeta. Many wore school uniforms: dark blue or brown, high school badges embroidered on their caps. Everyone knew where he belonged.

No one had died in the city of my birth since the sun had gone beyond recall, and no one had had new garments made. Their uniformlike clothes were not quite tattered yet, not by any means; but they reminded one of the costumes of a theater wardrobe worn over and over for many performances; somewhat graying at the seams, somewhat fraying at the cuffs, stale smells buried in each fold. And yet, such clean people. Clean as smoke.

I seemed to require no sleep or food in the city of my birth, but only speech. Now I have slept, I told myself, now I have eaten, and it would be as though I had slept and eaten and could go on. And on and on I went, through the dark streets, only some of which I remembered, and some of which were ruined and not repaired but closed.

One night I drove to the opera in a carriage. The horse defecated as it went, but the odor of the dung did not reach me. I realized all of a sudden that there were no smells in this city. The coachman wore an old battered top hat, and when I paid my fare he raised his hat in greeting and cracked his whip in a special way, an expert crack in the air. He knew me for a visitor, but he did not know that I came from the land of the sun. Perhaps he did not know about that land at all, though it was so near, right beyond the wall, only a password between the twilight and it. Most people do not know.

At the opera I met the man I married that night, that year. They were singing Mozart on stage, and the audience was so pleased, so responsive, that at times it seemed audience and singers might be interchangeable. I myself, I imagine, could have gone up there and joined the singer in "Voi chè sapete." There was a festive mood about it all, an air of goodwill, bravo, bravo, rows of women's hats bobbing joyously, how can one live without Mozart.

The man sitting by my side at the opera leaned over and said:

"We must leave in the intermission, quickly, because the opera will be surrounded by soldiers after the performance and this whole audience taken away to freight trains."

I consented, though wondering how come all these people knew it and none escaped. In the intermission the man took my hand and we left quickly by a side door. Trucks with bored soldiers were already posted in the square, the soldiers preparing to get off and surround the building. Their sergeants, papers in hand, were checking the order of deployment. A young soldier was whistling "Voi chè sapete" and said to his fellow, "How can one live without Mozart?"

In the dark light, the no-light, I asked the man holding my hand without my feeling its touch why people weren't escaping, and he said:

"Why, this whole thing repeats itself each night."

He drew me over to a door, narrow as a servants' entrance, and through it to a slippery, winding staircase, mounting to a roof. The roof was very peculiar: we were standing at the altitude of an airplane's flight, perhaps twelve thousand feet, perhaps more, very high. Yet I could see every single detail in the opera square below.

The floodlights of the soldiers' trucks came on suddenly, tearing the darkness, glaring and terrible, and with this evil light came the wails, the shouts, and the curses. Now everything happened fast. The people in their festive clothes piled up on the trucks, and there was no more telling them apart, batch after driven batch. Only the soldiers stood out clearly, because they were shouting so.

"Operation Cauldron," said the man by my side. "Every night it repeats itself. Every night they are driven in trucks like that to the trains and do not return. Next evening they are back, going to the opera, and it all starts over again. The only difference is that the people are a little less alive each time. They fade, like pictures in an album. But the process is so slow it is barely noticeable."

"And you — don't they take you in Operation Cauldron?" I asked.

"No," he said, "I'm already . . . " and stopped with a wave of the hand. Then he added: "You don't have to go either. Of course, if you want to . . . "

The moment he said that I was seized by a whirlwind. I wanted, wanted unto death to leap from this tall roof into the dark courtyard now filled with shouting soldiers, to go out to the opera square. Together with all the children. Together with all the neighbors, whom now I suddenly recognized one by one, Mrs. Paula and Mr. Arkin and his wife, and Moshe of the haberdashery who used to give me pictures of angels and cherubs to stick in my copybooks, and Bolek the druggist's son. They were all being herded onto the trucks here before my eyes, fearful and apprehensive, the soldiers shouting over their heads. And I wished to leap and be with them. To be taken.

"I did not leap either," said the man, very sad, as though confessing a sin. The whirlwind began to abate. I held on to the parapet and breathed hard. A fierce desire had come and gone and left me reeling.

One by one the trucks moved off with a terrible jarring noise. In the square lay a child's ballet slipper, a gilt-knobbed walking stick, and an ostrich feather from the hat of a lady in the opera audience. Then they *are* somewhat diminished each night, I thought to myself, and my anxiety found no relief. The emptiness that remained in the square had drained my body to the core.

"Tomorrow it will all happen again," said the man by my side. Grief was everywhere. It was all over.

"Could we get married?" I asked, like someone asking permission to take a vacant chair in a café.

And he nodded and said: "We could, yes."

*W*e did not know where we should live. All that night we wandered through the streets, as there was no telling day from night except for a slight shade of difference in the depth of darkness; everything was shrouded in the same no-light of the extinguished city. That night we also crossed a park, which since the sun had gone had long ceased being a park; many marble statues were strewn over the ground now, statues of people, some of them smashed. One small statue was very like my grandfather. I wanted to take it away with me, but I had no place to put it. Once or twice I also saw a white marble statue of a horse, its haunch wrenched off and something like frozen blood on the marble. There had not been so many statues in my childhood days, not just in the park but all over town. They had apparently turned the park into a dump, maybe for all the world. The presence of the kind people from the streets was missing here, and we returned to the city that never slept, that always had men and women walking about, huddled against the cold— till we got to a smoky alehouse. A few people, their breath misty in the cold air, their spirits high, were crowded in the doorway but did not go in.

The man with me briefly considered entering the place, then as quickly dismissed the idea. There was a space behind the alehouse, a kind of small courtyard paved with concrete, and in it a tiny shed, which I took for an outhouse. He opened its door and we went in; but there was no end to the shed, and its far side had another

door, behind which lay, suddenly, a vast deserted resi-
dence. It had heavy, very rich furniture, a sideboard and
carpets and enormous armchairs, and crystal chandeliers
thick with dust and cobwebs. I had always known that
this house existed behind some wall or other, and that
one day I would inherit it. Generations of my forefathers
must have lived here, they and their wives, my grandmothers in their handsome bonnets. I went in, un-
amazed. The furniture was too large and unwieldy, and
we decided we would use only one of the rooms, a plain
and all but empty one with a kind of stove on the floor
to be stoked with paper or wood. The man crouched and
lit a fire, the heat of which I did not feel, and his shadow
fell across me. I accepted what was to be. He blew on the
fire a little, and when it was going somehow, he checked
the window locks, then stood before me and said:

"The wedding took place this afternoon."

I knew these words to be our wedding rites and I was
very still, the way one is on solemn occasions. This will
be my life from now on, I told myself, in a city without
light, perhaps one day the soldiers will come for me too,
take me to the trucks, the trains, along with all of them,
with all of them, with all of them. I shall say to all the
children: Wait for me. I shall say: I am coming with you,
of course I am coming with you.

All at once the room filled with people, women in
shawls, neighbors. They came beaming, bearing gifts,
cases, cartons. They all stood squeezed in the doorway,
in the room, filling it, joyously offering their blessings in
identical words: the wedding took place this afternoon,
they said and kissed me, the wedding took place this afternoon. The room overflowed with people and with
parcels. I opened one, and it held all the toys I had lost

as a child and never found. The neighbor who had brought them stood over me, smiling, angelic, and repeated excitedly, the wedding took place this afternoon. She knew that her present was apt.

Afterward the neighbor women left, their thin voices, fluttery with a small, birdlike gladness, trailing down the staircase, and all the parcels remained: cases and cartons and beribboned boxes. I saw no need to shift them, though they hardly left us space to move about the room.

"This is where we shall live," I told the man in the room with me, and he nodded his head in assent.

So a year went by. We lived like lizards, in crevices, among the empty cases in the room. I do not remember anyone buying food, but every day I crossed the long corridor, past the large, imposing, unheated, and unlived-in rooms, to cook something in a kitchen that was like a large cave. Once we even went on an outing. Behind our apartment, not on the alehouse side but on the other, lay a desert stretching for many miles, and beyond the desert, in the distant haze, a range of mountain peaks, very far away. We stood at the edge of the house, a few dozen others with us, and looked at those faraway hills.

"Where is that?" I asked the people with us. They grinned good-naturedly and would not tell me, as though I should have known.

One of them said: "Los Angeles," but that was a joke.

I went in, back to our room, took off my shoes, my feet weary as after a long walk.

Now and then we would hear shouts from one of the

nearby houses: the soldiers come for the kill. They never got to us. We would lie numb, waiting for the night's Operation Cauldron to end, the leaden silence to return, the hollow grief.

Toward the end of the year I gave birth. The child tore away from me at one stroke; and I remembered dimly that once, long ago, in my other life, I had loved a man very much, and it was just this way I had felt when he tore away from my body: as though a part of me had suddenly been separated for all time. Then I wept many tears.

The child stood up and walked within a day or two. Next he began talking to me, demanding something, in an incoherent speech I failed to understand; he grew angry, and I knew he would not stay with me long. One day he left and did not return. When the man came home he removed his coat wordlessly and we both knew: the child had run off to the opera square. And it had been impossible to prevent.

The days went by, day running into night without any real difference between them. Sometimes kindhearted neighbors called. Once one of them came with scraps of material, a dressmaker's leftovers; we spent a whole morning sewing children's frocks, except that at the end of the day we had to unravel them all.

One day I knew that time had come full circle: my year in the city without light was over and I was to go back. I said to the man with me:

"I'm going."

He nodded. He did not offer to come with me. I would have to fall asleep in order to wake up in the other country anyway, and he could not accompany me into sleep. I think we never slept once in all that year, neither he nor I. Our eyelids were always open, day and night.

I lay down on my bed, which only now turned out to have wheels like a hospital bed, and the man I was with set it going with one hard shove along the corridor, which turned into a steep incline, and the bed rolled into the kitchen. The kitchen, where all that year I had gone to cook, had changed: it had been set up as an operating room. I was not surprised. I lay there waiting, unafraid. All the instruments were apparently ready; only the big lamp above me was still unlit. A stern-faced surgeon in a green coat and cap bent over me, examined me at a glance, and said:

"Turn on the light."

The big lamp blazed over my head, and I fell into a heavy sleep and woke up in my other house.

*I*t was morning. A great sun shone straight into my eyes. Ailanthus branches gently swayed on the veranda, drawing curtains of light whisper-soft across my face. A rich smell of coffee hung in the air, but as yet I could not take deep breaths of it. My soul did not return to me at once.

Through the door came the murmurs of my husband's and children's voices, speaking softly so as not to wake me. I cherished them but could not understand them from within yet, as though they were a translation that had not come off well. I lay still, waiting for my soul to flow full in me again, and I knew it was all over and completed: I would no more go back to the city of my birth, to the lightless city. Dante's verse dimmed, faded, returned to the pages of the book, a line like any other: its power exhausted. In a day or two I might even be able to read it without a pang. And sleep too, I told myself wonderingly, to be able really to sleep. My past was commuted. From now on I would find nothing there but the stones of Jerusalem, and plants growing with mighty vigor, and a vast light.

I got up to make breakfast, my heart beating hard.

Translated by Miriam Arad

Loneliness

*M*rs. Dolly Jacobus, who in recent years had arrived at a sure and sedate self-love, sat at her desk pondering how to finish a letter. It was a letter to her husband. All morning long she had basked in the fact that he was at an architects' conference in Malta and that she could write him there, write the word *Valletta,* which had such a light and chivalrous sound that it made her think of a young, robed knight quickly dismounting and elegantly stripping off his riding gloves: *Valletta.* Not until she had sat down to write did the reality become too much for her: what really did she know about such places, or about the space, proper or outlandish, that Meir Jacobus occupied in them? She could never imagine her husband once she was no longer by his side. Perhaps he had a different existence then, a different face.

Mrs. Dolly Jacobus took her pen and continued to write:

It is 10 A.M. now. Lots of light strikes the desk through the branches of the big olive tree. Do you remember how uncertain I was whether you had planned the window correctly? It seemed so high. But I'm glad of it now: there's just the right amount of light at just the right times. It's a lovely house, Meir. When I go to town and come back — and I don't go that often, because it's still been very rainy, and between one rain and the next the whole city is out in the streets trying to catch up on its affairs — it seems to me that someone has been in the house and has managed to slip away while I was still on the stairs. I look in the mirror and try to make out who it was. Perhaps it's a sign that you're thinking of me and the house. If you're planning to bring me a lace scarf from Malta, please bring a golden, white, or ivory one, and, in any event, not black. And since I have no idea how you're managing your time there, let me remind you of the advice that you once gave me: Surtout, pas trop de zèle. *Adieu, my dear friend.*

She quickly reread the letter: yes, it would pass muster beneath her husband's finely critical eye. There were no annoying questions in it of the how-are-you? when-are-you-coming-back? variety, no burdensome I-miss-you, or it's-so-difficult-without-you. Meir Jacobus had taught her long ago that an undue concern for the practical arrangements of life was a distinctly plebeian trait. Within a year or two of their marriage she had learned not to ask what would be. What will be, will be, he would quietly answer her. Sometimes, taking pity on her anxiousness, he would add, "In the station that you've reached, Dolly, you can afford to be impractical."

Mrs. Dolly Jacobus took a long envelope, sealed the letter inside it, and addressed it to the hotel in Valletta in a slightly slanting hand. Her handwriting was unusual: the letters were long, tall, personal, somewhat squared at the edges, as though she had practiced developing a private calligraphy of her own. Only her signature was small and crumpled, a shelter within a shelter within a shelter. A graphologist had once frightened her with the opinion that it was a drawing of a fetus in the womb. Four consecutive miscarriages of indeterminable cause left her without children and with the perpetual irritation of an impatient soul that strives for wholeness and cannot understand why it has not come, what can be taking it so long? Only in recent years had this irritation begun to wane. It was with a measure of optimism that she now looked after her home, her husband, and her many flowerpots. She regarded herself in the mirror with a satisfied if slightly critical air. She went to lectures at the university, where she had her favorite professors whom she never missed, and her passing academic friendships with smiles across rows of chairs, banter between classes.

Self-love had descended on her slowly, by degrees; it had grown securely out of that greater, more comprehensive love that she had felt for her beautiful home, her books, her paintings, her expensive shoes (which were too elegant to be of Israeli mold), her restaurants, her credit cards (yes, Mrs. Jacobus, of course, Mrs. Jacobus), her view of the walled Old City of Jerusalem on which the windows of her house looked down. Dolly Jacobus considered this view to be a private performance put on in her behalf, which she would watch from her gallery in all its many aspects of time and light. Once a visiting friend from the university had sat at the wide window bathed in Herodean light and asked after a long silence:

"Do you mean to tell me that you can go on looking

out on all this every hour of the day without feeling anxious?"

Dolly Jacobus lifted and dropped one shoulder.

"And you can just go on looking down on all this?" the visitor asked again wonderingly. "Just looking down?"

"I must be a butterfly," said Dolly Jacobus. Her face broke into the lopsided grin that helped make her so likable. "But I want you to know," she added, "that being a butterfly is something that I have to work at very hard."

She was too rich for anyone to feel really sorry for her, yet people still said "poor Dolly" when they mentioned her. Nobody knew why. A year before, she had taken up batik and made gifts of her many creations, but the dyeing proved too messy for her and she gave it up in the end. Instead she tried writing haiku. She would in fact have sent her husband a few pithy haiku right now in lieu of a letter, but for her fear that the poems might travel poorly and spoil in the course of their flight over the unnecessarily large ocean that separated her from Meir. All a person really needed in the way of room, she had once thought to herself, were three or four streets around him. Only someone who had never been a refugee could dare dream of oceans and great expanses of space. And twenty-five years ago Dolly Jacobus had been a refugee. To this day she was astonished by such things as central heating, which kept on burning warmly, really burning, while the rain remained outside. Truly outside, it wasn't just an optical illusion.

It transpired that she was out of postage stamps, and since she had planned a trip to a delicatessen downtown anyway, she decided to go.

Settling into her small car, she reached into the glove

compartment and took out a pair of embroidered house shoes in which she preferred to drive. With her feet in the soft slippers, the car itself became a kind of private room. The rearview mirror showed her a pointed, attractive face with the barest hint of — not that she actually had the beginnings of one, but the skin above her lips was a trifle darker than elsewhere, so that in all her photographs she was obliged to have it lightened — a mustache over her upper lip. Dolly adjusted the mirror and turned the key in the ignition. To her satisfaction, the motor started at once despite the cold weather.

The city sped toward her in a rush of confusion. People had trouble deciding whether to open their umbrellas or close them: those who opened them had them blown inside-out like a funnel by the wind, while those who closed them were liable to be drenched by a sudden gust of rain. Both groups hurried impatiently, lengthening a stride to avoid a puddle or shortening one against a blast of wind. The hair of the women blew wildly; here and there a young girl ran giggling to catch a kerchief that had flown away. Dark patches of rain stained the walls of the houses. Blotchy clouds sped through the sky between the roofs, through which at irregular intervals the sun struggled to appear. Children were sailing a paper boat in a dirty puddle. A gray truck, whose driver seemed lost in thought, drove right through it, spraying grimy water mixed with bits of paper in every direction. The city stone seemed dim and weary. The whole street smelled disagreeably of wet dog fur. For a minute Dolly contemplated turning back to shelter within the clean, warm comfort of her house with its central heating that burned, really burned, cheerily all the time. But she had already come too far.

She parked in a lot downtown. Meir Jacobus's office was
nearby, on the top floor of one of the new sharp sky-
scrapers that seemed determined in their hatred of the
city to get as high above it as they could. No private individual would ever build such a thing for himself; people did such things in groups to get rich quickly from the
city. The contracting firm that built this particular building also employed its guards and maintenance staff, as
well as the attendants in the nearby parking lot. Once,
while having her car washed, it was whispered by one of
them in Mrs. Jacobus's ear that the firm was not on the
up-and-up, and even shortchanged its employees in their
paychecks. For a while she thought of doing something
about it; after all, people should have a union that will
press their demands. Not that she knew the first thing
about it, far from it, but these were matters that everyone
read about in the newspaper: workers had unions and
even went out on strike. It upset her to see people ill-
treated, and she raised the subject one day in Meir's
office. It was afternoon, and she had come to drive him
home. His sister and partner, Bilhah, an architect herself
and a triple divorcée with an exaggeratedly svelte body
and a passion for jewelry, was there too. Almost apologetically, Dolly Jacobus murmured something about ex-
ploitation, about overtime, something about unions.

Bilhah glanced up from her drafting paper, her
bracelets and bangles coolly silent, and said:

"Really, Dolly, I don't know why on earth you
should want to be such a public-service bus."

Dolly didn't want to be a public-service bus. She
dropped the subject. Still, something of the goodwill she
felt remained with her, something of that indefinable
sympathy that everyone can sense even if no one can put

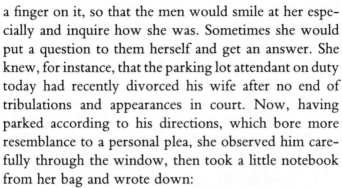
a finger on it, so that the men would smile at her especially and inquire how she was. Sometimes she would put a question to them herself and get an answer. She knew, for instance, that the parking lot attendant on duty today had recently divorced his wife after no end of tribulations and appearances in court. Now, having parked according to his directions, which bore more resemblance to a personal plea, she observed him carefully through the window, then took a little notebook from her bag and wrote down:

"The divorced man: his shirt more pressed than usual (laundries), his shoulders more hunched than usual (restaurants)."

Her notebook and the insight that went into it improved her mood. She considered herself an astute observer. Dolly has a keen eye, she often remarked to herself. She snapped her bag shut as the attendant approached the car window: good morning, madam, how are you today, would you like the car washed? She flashed the broad smile that she reserved for her faithful followers, no, thank you, the car won't be here long enough, you know how forgetful I am, really, I don't know what I'd do without you. As she talked, she felt that she was overdoing it, saying and smiling too much. Meir would have got the same message across with two words and a short wave of his hand. The attendant too was confused and didn't know whether to stay or leave. Was there something else the lady wished to say to him? Luckily, another car entered the lot at that moment and saved him from his predicament.

Dolly locked the car door and made a mental note to give the man a gift for his politeness on the first available holiday. Indeed, Purim was next week: perhaps some imported deodorant would do. It was a pity how few people in this perspiring land understood the importance of deodorant. Such a gift would be both practical and pleasurable. Yet, Dolly Jacobus was far from a brainless woman: what would happen, she asked herself, when the supply of expensive deodorant was used up? The parking lot attendant had alimony to pay and certainly could not afford such luxuries, while she and Meir could hardly supply him with deodorant forever — a can every holiday, or perhaps even every week, how absurd. In the meantime the sun reappeared, and the clouds in Dolly's mind dispersed too. She would give it to him this once and take her chances. What was so wrong with making a man happy just once? Life was all ups and downs anyway.

Having withstood the temptation to succumb this time too to an undue concern for practical arrangements, which was always a source of anxiety, her mood improved even more. Dolly Jacobus was an orderly woman who didn't like to leave problems unsolved, not even the bare thought of one. She smoothed out her dress and walked to the building. A silent elevator took her quickly to the top floor, where her husband's office was.

The door was open. Bilhah was inside by herself, bent over some tracing paper with a compass. She was always bent over something. A low desk lamp cast an intense pool of light on the table, in which Bilhah's rings bubbled as though being brought to a boil.

"Oh, it's you," said Bilhah Jacobus unenthusiastically. Her rings fell silent for a moment, then started to bubble again.

"Are you alone? Where's Esther?"

Esther was the secretary, a tall, ugly, unpleasant, gum-chewing girl who wore a wig made of someone else's hair and had never learned to answer the telephone properly. Moreover, she didn't need the job, nor did Meir and Bilhah really need a secretary; but her parents, of a prominent Jerusalem family that had two or three different marriage ties with the Jacobus family, had pleaded for her.

"Esther has been working so hard all year long," said Bilhah sarcastically, "that she decided to take a vacation. Now that Meir is away, she thought she had one coming to her."

"Maybe she did."

Bilhah threw her a mocking look that left nothing out or unalluded to, from Esther's glum, gum-chewing slow-wittedness, to the niggardly, have-pity-on-me vibrations that she gave off. Before such realities Dolly Jacobus could not but bow down. In Meir's and Bilhah's tolerance of Esther, it seemed to her, was a certain hypocrisy, a kind of mock stoicism that was too much for her to understand.

"What are you doing now, Bilhah?"

"The same as before Meir took off."

"What's that?"

"Entrances for Zone Three of the Jewish Quarter. Didn't Meir tell you?"

Bilhah knew perfectly well that Meir never told her anything.

"Show me."

But Bilhah placed her hand over the paper.

"There's nothing to see yet. You wouldn't understand it anyway."

Each time Dolly felt all over again how out of place she was in this office, which was Meir's workaday world. Whenever she telephoned and was answered by Esther's wooden voice, her depression was so great that she couldn't remember what she had called to say. More than once she had actually forgotten some urgent matter and hadn't dared call back again. It was like standing by a sea rail and watching things fall from one's hands into the water, irretrievable.

"I'm going to the post office now, Bilhah. Is there anything urgent for Meir?"

"Look on his desk" came the indifferent reply. Bilhah returned to her measurements. Two heavy bracelets jangled on her wrist.

Dolly Jacobus went over to the window, which wasn't a real window but an immovable panel of glass. The sight of the bare, unshaded light bulb burning in the broad daylight of the room made her uneasy. There was something abnormal, something hybrid and unlifelike about it, almost a sin against those natural processes that have their own relaxed flow. This dizzying, too high, too enclosed, eternally air-conditioned room with its hermetically sealed windows and its strong lamplight at eleven o'clock in the morning, when a premature spring wind was whirling outside, disturbed her peace of mind and all but depressed her. She felt the need to get outside into the fresh air and leaves, where from time to time an unmistakable gust from the south would pierce the galloping whirlpool of air, flaring the nostrils with keen desert desire—a southern breeze such as could only be felt in Jerusalem in autumn and spring. To get away, away, to gallop quickly, to give oneself away.

Nothing of this could be felt in the office. Bilhah Jacobus was confined to her white beam of light, from which she declared:

"There's something there from Grandma Haya that Meir hasn't seen yet. She commands us to wall in the windows in her dining room that face out onto the new housing projects. She says that she can't stand to look at them, that each time she sees how they've ruined her mountain, her blood pressure goes up."

There was always some new story about Grandma Haya that was told with the same helpless affection. Grandma Haya was a monument, and monuments are a law unto themselves. She was eighty-nine years old, though she confessed to only eighty-seven, and still cooked all her holiday specialties for daughters-in-law, who—poor things!—had no strength of their own. Once she paid a royal visit to Dolly and Meir's house, where she sat for a long time at the broad window that looked down on the Old City. Yes, yes, she said. It all belonged to her. She could look out on it all, she who had never been a young starving refugee with a funny family name that had to be changed in a new land. Grandma Haya appraised Dolly sternly and asked if there were roaches in her kitchen.

"No, Grandma Haya, there aren't," said Dolly, hiding a smile.

Grandma Haya declared firmly:

"I congratulate you."

Meir and Bilhah's grandmother lived in an old house

full of arches with an outdoor toilet she used day and
night, summer and winter, and refused to exchange for
a modern, indoor one such as Meir and Bilhah had been
begging her to install for years. The rooms of her house
were abrasively spotless, cleaner than clean, with their
white curtains, whiter tablecloths, and heavy silver
candlesticks polished to such a brilliance that they
seemed to shine even at night. In his childhood, Meir
claimed, he had been afraid to sleep in the same room
with the candlesticks because of their light. Each time he
awoke, he thought he was seeing a thief's flashlight.

One wall of Grandma Haya's bedroom was covered
with a large map of the world in which were stuck little
flags. Grandma Haya was a sixth-generation Jerusalemite, she had grandchildren and great-grandchildren all
over the globe, and she wanted to know exactly where
each one of them was. An orange flag with the name
Nurit on it was thrust into London. A bright blue flag
that said Elisha and Tali was near Tel Aviv. There was
a reddish flag for Yoav somewhere in Sinai.

Not that Yoav ever served in Sinai, but Grandma
Haya assumed that if he was in the army, it could only
be there. She had once been in Sinai herself with her
departed husband, the doctor, on an expedition of En-
glishmen, and had ridden sidesaddle, as was the custom
of ladies in those days. Her memories of the trip — more
portraiture, really, than memory — were of ravens, cliffs,
and untold dangers. Perhaps vague longings for the place
lingered on, for why else would she so staunchly insist
that Yoav was there when he wasn't, braving all those

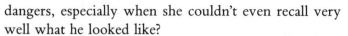
dangers, especially when she couldn't even recall very well what he looked like?

Grandma Haya was distressed that so few of her flags were in Jerusalem, while in the United States alone there were three, one belonging to Adi, who had been married there in a Catholic church. At first Grandma Haya had wanted to pull that flag out of her map, but at the last minute she relented, so that it remained crookedly in place as though it did not quite belong. Dolly clearly remembered the moment nearly twenty years ago when Grandma Haya had risen from her seat and planted in the heart of Jerusalem a lemon-colored flag that said Meir and Dolly on it. They had already been married two weeks at the time, but to all of them this seemed the real wedding. At last Dolly had come home. The bare, goaty hill outside the window had seemed to her a potential disaster area of which she alone was afraid. Now that her flag stood firmly in Grandma Haya's map, she felt that she too could relax.

*D*olly Jacobus stood in her husband's office and pressed her head against the storm-beaten, forever-sealed window; Bilhah sat in the strong beam of light silently swearing at some unsuccessful calculation, her jewelry coming slowly to a boil again; and up on her hillside Grandma Haya sat at home, furious at the intruding housing projects that had put her old age to shame. For once in her life she too had no strength to fight back.

*T*here was a long line of people in the post office. The fan on the ceiling wasn't working. At the head of the line stood a messenger boy from some office with several dozen registered letters. As soon as he finished, two soldiers advanced out of turn and demanded to be served. The post office kept growing more packed; it was as though half the city had decided to crowd into it, each person with many items to mail. The clerk at the window was slow and incompetent; complaints began to be heard. Dolly Jacobus would gladly have left, but she was already nearer to the front of the line than to the rear, and to elbow her way back out through the dense crowd seemed harder than waiting her turn. Perspiration formed on her forehead.

Directly in front of her stood a very small teenage girl with the emaciated, almost monkeylike appearance of a stunted child. Only her chest and her buttocks stuck out sharply like false appendages that didn't quite belong to her. There was something pitifully sharp and shrunken about her, as though privation had caused her to stop growing in the womb; she seemed more a homunculus than a grown person—a snuffed-out, lightless little candle. A strong smell of the cheapest violet-scented perfume came from her body, together with an odor of cigarettes and sweat. No doubt the perfume took the place of daily baths; very likely she slept in her clothes. Amid the great press of people, her curly hair was thrust right beneath Mrs. Dolly Jacobus's nose. She wore tiny doll-like blue jeans that were slightly open at the waist and a shiny purple blouse from some bargain stand. Where the two failed to meet, a strip of naked, pathetically lackluster skin was exposed, on which grew a dark tuft of animal-like hair. She looked concentrated, smoky, and bad. Her neck was unwashed.

In the girl's hands, Mrs. Jacobus saw, were two reg-

istered letters from the law office of Advocate Yitzhaki
on Ben-Yehuda Street. Dolly Jacobus and her husband
knew Yitzhaki well and had often visited his large home
in the German Colony quarter, which somehow made
the girl seem less a stranger to her. With her usual avidity
to be liked by her inferiors, or perhaps out of a loneliness
so habitual that she no longer even sensed that it was
there, she smiled encouragingly at the girl. The complaints and congestion had grown worse, if such a thing
were imaginable, and Dolly Jacobus sought to free herself of them by moving forward a bit, when she suddenly
realized to her astonishment that the dark-skinned waif
of a girl not only failed to move too, but deliberately
seemed to press backward and turn her head, so that her
dark mouth unmistakably delved like an inquisitive kitten's against the soft silk bodice covering Mrs. Dolly
Jacobus's right breast. A current of rare flame shot
through Dolly's body and, with it, an indistinct fear. She
sought to move away once more, which was far from
easy in the great throng of people, which had long ceased
to preserve even the semblance of a line. This time, however, there was no possibility of error: the girl pressed
against Dolly Jacobus's stomach as though in an open
and explicit invitation. She could feel the burning,
monkeylike heat of her seemingly chronically feverish
body. All of a sudden the girl looked up and regarded
Mrs. Dolly Jacobus with a sharp, clairvoyant impudence.

A hot wave, heavy, tropical, and damp, passed over
Dolly Jacobus. She jerked back her hand so as not to
touch the girl's waist and offendedly clamped her mouth
shut. Yet she knew, with a weak, sinking feeling, that she
could no longer resist the wave of desire rising, illimit-
ably shameless, within her. Not that she was unaware of

the element of sadism in this sudden new passion, of her
need to trample, to assail. But the girl appeared not to
mind, appeared to size up the situation exactly, with an
omniscience as old as the world. Compared to her, I'm
an amateur, Dolly Jacobus thought to herself, a rank amateur. She shut her eyes, conscious that in another moment she would move closer to the knowing little body
of her own accord. Just then, however, the post office
manager sent a clerk to open a second window; the line
melted away, and the girl stepped forward with her registered letters as though nothing had happened. She
mailed them and left the post office without looking at
Mrs. Jacobus.

*D*olly Jacobus put stamps on the letter to Valletta, which
was no longer a knight or even a geographical place but
simply a sound. She bought a few extra stamps and
dropped the letter in the mailbox, as though glad to be
rid of it. When she turned to look for her, the girl had already disappeared among the passersby and been swallowed up by the street. Dolly Jacobus retraced her steps
toward the parking lot, entered a dimly lit café on the
way, drank something hurriedly, and thought that the
storm had subsided. Yet when she turned onto Ben-
Yehuda Street she felt suddenly so faint, and the slope of
the sidewalk seemed so steep, that she feared she would
have to negotiate it on all fours. How, she wondered,
could everyone else be taking such a precipitous drop in
stride? I will never make it to the bottom, she said nearly
out loud to herself. Hesitantly she began to walk step by
step to her car, when she chanced to meet an acquaintance, a tall, merry young student from the university

wrapped in a duffle coat against the errant wind, who mercifully accompanied her part of the way. By the time he took his leave with seven-league strides, she was feeling better, sorry to see him go.

Dolly Jacobus had often wondered about the meaning of home. There were so many homes in the world, so many houses, and out of them all each person had one alone in which he knew where everything was. Of all the hundreds of thousands of homes, she thought, there is one alone to which I have the key and know that in the top drawer of the chest in the bedroom to the left is a tan camel's-hair sweater; of all the impenetrable, anonymous houses there is only one in which I can find right away the set of dishes that Meir brought from Spain. The lighter. The broom. The wash-and-dry sheets. Now, however, as she sat motionless in her car, she was no longer so sure of this nexus of knowledge between her and her house. If she were to return to it this minute, she felt, the key might not fit the door, so that she would remain trapped outside in impersonal space. And if it did fit, her memories might not. The sweater might not be in its drawer, and who knew whether the chest would be there at all; whether a different table would not be standing in place of the one she knew; whether the whole familiar house would not turn out to have been a dream, and the house she returned to a strangely furnished place that she had never arranged. Instead of her rosebushes there might be a strip of concrete on which an electric generator clanked away intolerably. Perhaps a gang of workers. Perhaps the house had been condemned already without her knowing it.

She ran a hand over her forehead to drive the nightmare away. It wasn't the first such ghastly vision she had had in the past two or three weeks. Several times she had dreamed that a stranger, someone she should have known but somehow was unable to recognize, had broken into her house; struggling with the hideous, mocking secret of who it was, she had broken free each time with a choked little cry. Now she was alone, and it was hard waking by herself in the middle of the night. Often she left the night-light on. Yet the panic underneath remained.

This is no good, Dolly Jacobus said to herself wonderingly, this is no good. Pulling herself together, she stuck the key in the ignition and decided to visit Grandma Haya.

If the weather outside was still behaving strangely, none of it was noticeable in Grandma Haya's house, which had a weather all its own. Meir had once remarked that Grandma Haya was the last ecological person in the family. She would never have dreamed of buying parsley and other herbs; she grew them herself, planted by the fig tree and the lemon tree in the courtyard. The idea, Grandma said, of buying a lemon in the store. The balsam with which she scented her linen closet was picked by her in the hills, or by one of her granddaughters when her back hurt too much to go look for it. An egg was a meal for her, and who could explain to her, pray, why people ran around as they did nowadays and caused themselves all kinds of diseases of the liver and the heart? People don't live by human proportions anymore, she would say: they build too high, live too high, and talk too high. It's an insult to creation. Offices, everyone must have an office.

It was indeed Meir's and Bilhah's good fortune that she had never been to their office, because if she had, who knew whether she wouldn't have taken a stick to them on account of the unopenable windows, fraudulent windows, an arrogance of a building. Once, when she went to town to buy fabric for a dress, Grandma Haya took one look at the prices and threw the cloth back on the counter. The nerve of you, she said to the salesgirl. The nerve of you. Then and there she swore that she would never buy another thing until impudence passed from the world. Over her dead body would the speculators get rich. Several years earlier she had gone to Tel Aviv and returned in a rage; ever since, her favorite phrase of dismissal was to say, that's from Tel Aviv. If someone brought her a box of chocolates, all becellophaned and beribboned, she would purse her mouth sarcastically and ask: is that from Tel Aviv? And once, when Dolly had brought her a book by some young author, she had declared after reading it: it must be from Tel Aviv. It was common knowledge that you didn't bring Grandma Haya flowers unless you had grown them in your own garden. Flower butchers was her name for flower shops.

In the middle of the Yom Kippur War, when she had grown tired of baking cakes for the soldiers, Grandma Haya decided to step out: she had an urge to go see the Chagall stained glass windows at Hadassah Hospital. Buses either came in those days or they didn't; over half an hour later Dolly found her sitting on the stone bench of the bus station and suggested that she take a taxi. What are you thinking of, child? Grandma Haya scolded her. Besides which, taxis were built low, you couldn't see anything out of them. Buses were built high, at least you could look out and see.

Grandma Haya no longer stepped out. She was tired, tired in that quiet way that marks the end of all wanting, of even the hint of a desire. I'm not afraid to die, she told her family. I've never quarreled with my body and I don't intend to quarrel with it now.

"Come on in," she said to Dolly with a bright smile, opening the door for her, "you can help me slice string beans in the kitchen." Grandma Haya never sliced string beans the lazy way, across. She always sliced them lengthwise, her knife passing right through the seeds in the pod. It gave them an entirely different taste.

They were seated opposite the black grandfather clock in the kitchen. Through the short, starched muslin curtains the light filtered in. Dolly had no idea why she had come. If it was to bare her heart, she herself wasn't sure what there was to bare. There was an opaqueness in her that she failed to comprehend but that kept her from returning home. She was in that state of blind anticipation in which one vaguely senses that things have come to a head, without knowing exactly what things or what head. Grandma Haya sliced string beans and talked.

"Once when Menahem, may he rest in peace, was alive, two young yeshivah students came to see him one Saturday morning. '*Doktor, kumt.*' 'Where to?' asked Menahem. 'Our rabbi has had a heart attack.' Menahem was already halfway out of the house with his doctor's case when I decided to open my mouth. 'Just how do you expect him to come with you on the Sabbath?' I asked. 'He won't be able to drive his car down your streets.' 'Then let him walk,' said the students. 'Oh no,' I said, 'oh no. My husband is a man of more than seventy, and he's not going anywhere on foot.' 'Just a minute,' said one of the students to me, 'we'd better talk things over between us.' So they went outside and whispered a bit, psss, psss, psss, and then came back in. '*Doktor, kumt!*' 'How is he going?' I asked. 'In his car,' they said. 'But they throw stones in your streets at cars traveling on the Sabbath,' I said. '*Doktor, kumt,*' they said. 'Just let him drive slowly behind us, everything will be all right.'

"So he got into his car, may he rest in peace, which by then couldn't have gone very fast anyway, neither it nor he, and drove slowly behind the two students, who walked ahead of him shouting '*Shaa! Shaa!*' to their left and to their right. When Menahem reached the police barrier blocking traffic into their quarter, the police were fast asleep, they never dreamed that anyone would try driving a car into Mea She'arim on the Sabbath. By the time they woke up, the two students had moved the barrier and Menahem had driven through. A policeman ran after them in a state of shock, shouting, 'Hey, it's *Shabbes!*' So what did the two students do? They turned around to him and said '*Shaa!*' That's how Menahem drove into Mea She'arim on the Sabbath, with the two students *shaa*'ing all the *Shabbes*-criers. He examined the rabbi, gave him something to feel better, and came home. We had a good laugh over it."

"How did he get back out, with the students?"

"No, by himself."

"And what happened?"

"They stoned him, of course, what do you think? Dolly, you're younger than I am, throw out this garbage and put some water in the kettle. Where is Meir?"

"Meir is in Malta. At an architects' conference."

Grandma Haya made a face.

"Why on earth Malta? What can a man expect to find in Malta? When is he coming back?"

"I don't know," Dolly confessed. "He didn't say exactly. Perhaps next week."

Grandma Haya was annoyed.

"What kind of business is that? A husband goes off to Malta-shmalta and his wife doesn't even know when he's coming back. You're an idiotic generation. I suppose you don't even know what's written in your marriage contract. In a Jewish marriage contract it says that a husband mustn't go off to the end of the earth without first asking his wife's permission. Did Meir ask your permission?"

"I gave him permission, Grandma Haya," smiled Dolly, the old, habitual darkness in her heart. "And you know he would have gone without permission anyway. That's how men are." Suddenly she found the courage to add: "Don't you think it might be better if women didn't marry men at all? Perhaps what a woman really needs is another woman."

But Grandma Haya wouldn't hear of it and flapped her hands in distress:

"What sort of nonsense is that? Really, the things you people say. A woman needs a woman, *feh*. What is this, Tel Aviv?"

Dolly made a soft, sweeping gesture with her palms, as though gathering in with great gentleness the curly head in the post office, like gathering a flower. She rose to go.

"I'll pour you your tea, Grandma Haya, and then I'll be off. Please, you needn't get up."

Grandma Haya got up anyway. In the grave, she

said, is where I'll stop getting up to say good-bye to my guests. She kissed Dolly at the door with the cold lips of a person who no longer has much vital heat. "And tell Meir that I don't like this going off of his one bit. Besides which, I want him and Bilhah to close up my windows in the dining room. There's enough to do here in Jerusalem. What is he running all over the world for?"

Home, when Dolly returned to it, was warm and very clean and smelled unmistakably of comfort and wealth. She took off her coat and sat down at the table, exhausted in advance, as though some grim and unavoidable disaster awaited her and she hadn't the strength to begin. Soon, however, God knew from where, a sharp burst of energy ran through her: now, at once, this evening, she must understand everything about herself once and for all. It was time she knew. She rummaged through the closet, took out all the albums and began feverishly looking for the few rare snapshots of herself from her refugee days. None lit the faintest spark. She could not find herself in any of them. Perhaps, she thought, if only, if only I had some picture from my childhood, from the age of four or five, perhaps then. But such a picture was not to be had anywhere on earth. It was as if Dolly had been twice-born, and her first, perhaps truer, life had ended abruptly at the age of fourteen. Afterward another, post-diluvian life had begun, with its disguises and new names.

A great wave of sadistic compassion, a feeling not unlike that of a little child who plays lovingly with a doll and a minute later punishingly tears out its hair, cast the girl from the post office up inside her again. The shame of it, thought Dolly dry-mouthed, the wonderful shame of it. Why, I am practically in need of her. Already she was planning how the two of them would sit here, at this table, studying English together. Dolly would teach her patiently, yet sometimes not, losing her temper in a fit of erotic anger; and as the weather would be hot, and the air conditioning was out of order, the two would take off their blouses. They would wash each other in the shower. One more step and the girl would be hers, a gutterbird, scrawny and adroit.

After midnight the wave vanished as suddenly as it had come. That's the last of it, she thought tiredly, the absolute last of it. I almost made a terrible mistake. Thank God I got over it in time. The situations a person can get herself into, really. She left the night-light on, took a sleeping pill, and drifted off into a deep, obtuse sleep.

At ten o'clock the next morning, without knowing a minute beforehand what she was about to do, Dolly Jacobus settled vehemently into her car, slammed the door shut with pursed lips, and drove off with a violent grinding of her gears. She parked in the usual lot, which was attended that morning by a new, unfamiliar face, and walked with quick steps in the direction of Advocate Yitzhaki's office. In her panic that she might reconsider and change her mind, she nearly ran up the steps. The lawyer's office was composed of two rooms entered from an old, peeling corridor that also housed several other offices, as well as a bathroom with a gigantic old key in its door and a small cubicle in which an aged, immortal-looking man sat making tea and coffee for the office workers. The older he grew, it was said, the more polished were his copper trays and the dirtier the drinking glasses borne on them.

Dolly Jacobus was still examining the nameplates on the wall when the bathroom door swung open at the end of the corridor and the girl in the purple blouse emerged and stopped to turn the key twice behind her. She looked even tinier than she had yesterday in the post office. An ancient, wicked triumph shone in her eyes when she caught sight of Mrs. Jacobus. She stepped up to her, too concentrated a ball of impudence for one small girl.

"Would you like to come work for me?" asked Dolly Jacobus. She felt that her generally musical voice lacked all expression, was as toneless as a block of wood.

"Whaddam I gonna do fa' you?" asked the girl with a trace of scorn. "I ain't no cleaning woman. I work for a lawyer, y'know."

"I know that you do," said Mrs. Jacobus. "You're Advocate Yitzhaki's messenger girl. But wouldn't you like to get ahead in the world? I could teach you English if you'd like."

The girl stared at her blankly.

"It won't cost you a penny," said Dolly Jacobus. "You can come every day to study for an hour, an hour and a half."

The girl gave her head a skeptical shake.

"You'll be sorry y'ast." She seemed to hold the consonants and then spit them menacingly out of her mouth. Cheekily.

"Wouldn't you like to try?"

The girl looked at her askance. To do so she had to throw back her head, since Mrs. Jacobus was much taller.

From the girl came the smell of a recently chewed sesame bar.

"When do you finish working here?"

"Me? At six."

"Fine. Be down near the Agron building at six. I'll be waiting for you in my car."

"Me? I can't today. I gotta date with my boyfriend, see?"

So soon, so soon the degradation of it had begun. Dolly Jacobus could feel the knife that was being slowly, almost gently turned in her body. *Already I am at the mercy of her whims, of her boyfriend, who may or may not exist, most likely not.* A terrible pity flooded her eyes. She placed a gentle hand on the girl's cheek.

"All right, little girl. Let's make it tomorrow."

The girl must have had no idea of how to respond to an innocent touch, for immediately she thrust out her hips like a streetwalker's, as though it were expected of her. Dolly Jacobus swallowed a hot lump, turned on her heels, and began descending the stairs.

"Hey, missus!" called the girl after her, leaning over the balcony. "Missus! Listen, missus, it's okay. Let's make it today."

And Dolly Jacobus felt weak with happiness.

A letter was waiting for her at home from Meir, special delivery, as was his habit. She put off opening it. There were two telephone calls. A friend called to invite her and Meir to Friday night dinner, but said quickly when told that Meir was still away, all right, then, let's make it some other time, bye-bye, Dollinka, and send the man my best. Then Grandma Haya called, querulous, cross, and very old. Why wasn't Meir back yet? Why weren't her windows taken care of? Did they think she was going to live forever? She had completely forgotten Dolly's visit of yesterday.

Otherwise, there was nothing to do. Lust turned into a series of practical details: a meal ready in the refrigerator, plates on the table, a record that took a long time to choose, a new blouse that lay in its wrapper in the bedroom to give the girl as a gift. She had bought it in a children's store, since sizes that small were available nowhere else. Three times she went to town shopping and three times she came back. It all became so new, blind, and inevitable. Hurry, hurry.

*T*he Agron building was very white in the dusky light. Gray haze rose from the acacia trees to mingle with the exhaust of many cars, against which the lampposts and yellow fences stood out strongly. Dolly Jacobus felt everything intensify: all shapes seemed more significant—the white gleam of the stone that faced the office building, that streetlight over there that was making a simple statement—as though they were all in a code that had to be learned to be read. The cloud-dampened, haze-dimmed twilight did not surprise her: why, since last evening her world had been darkening—since well before last evening in fact—with that last eerie glow that portends a certain disaster. I am waiting for my love, she told herself, for my poor, ugly love with her smell of sweat and synthetic violets. To support her in the style she will become accustomed to. I shall not skimp.

She waited a long time. The girl did not appear. A gang of boys on their way to Morasha passed by her car and peered apathetically inside at her. A young mother screamed at her son with practiced, despairing, almost ceremonial screams. Two foreign journalists whom she knew waved at her on their way to the press club. Suddenly, in a gust of evening breeze, the acacias began to touch one another, to talk back and forth. The city whirled the evening around inside it, rings within rings; soon it would be suppertime, soon it would be nighttime, soon there would be streetlights and movies and people clustered around hot popcorn. The whirling rings slowly thickened into solid darkness. The girl had not come.

At seven o'clock, cold, beat, and aching, Dolly Jacobus pressed the accelerator and headed for home. What luck, she thought, at least she doesn't know my name and address, all I needed was to have a blackmail case on my hands, she and her boyfriend together, don't get wise with us, lady, we know all about you. Or some venereal disease, who knows. How could Yitzhaki even employ such a horrible girl? Why, one ought to . . . one ought to . . .

She hurried to enter the house, which seemed to her now all Meir's: those were his clothes in the closet, his slippers on the floor—what a disgrace, really, the things she had thought of doing in it—even the shirt from the children's store that lay on his side of the bed. Blushingly she took it and threw it in the garbage pail. I didn't do anything, Meir, she said to herself, I only thought of it—and thoughts aren't deeds, Meir, are they? She drew open the heavy curtain, which revealed the most stunning landscape on earth: the old walls of Jerusalem, the Temple Mount, and Mount Zion. It's all there, she reassured herself, it's still there, all those thousands of houses dipped now in darkness as though they, as though they alone, were the only true houses and deserved to have their wishes come true. She looked around her. The pictures still hung on the walls, the books hadn't vanished, her shoeless foot sunk as sensually as always into the Mashhad carpet, my God, how could I, how — the lunacy of it.

She suddenly made up her mind to call Meir. True, he had firmly, with all the authority of a rational man, warned her not to do it, so that she feared the moment of his anger and surprise — but she must hear his voice, if only to tell him about Grandma Haya's windows, or to find out the number of his return flight, just to talk. She explained to the long-distance operator that she did not know the number, but that she wanted to get the Hotel Phoenix in Valletta. Yes, Valletta, the capital of Malta, that's correct. Once again it seemed to her the most cavalier and elegant of cities. Yet it was hard for her to imagine Meir walking its streets without his car, since he had long ago turned into a centaur, part man and part automobile. It was perhaps only in bed that he sometimes still lay peeled of his layers and defenseless. Who knew what his strength was without his car in the streets of Valletta?

While waiting for the operator to call back, she prepared herself a sandwich, which she ate sitting on the arm of the easy chair, her bare feet crossed. Soon I will speak with Meir, she thought, I will hear the wonder in his voice — the same mild wonder I always hear, as though life itself was not what he had expected. Meir Jacobus, architect, a man who found it easier to talk about entrances for Zone Three of the Jewish Quarter than about what was going on inside him. We've drifted apart a bit lately, Meir, thought Dolly, but it will all work out, won't it? We will talk now and it will work out.

The sandwich was eaten. Dolly had just gone to the kitchen to get an apple when the telephone rang. She left the unwashed fruit by the sink and ran barefoot to the telephone.

The long-distance operator told her to wait. She heard her talking to the operator in Valletta. Then to the desk at the hotel. So many different voices talking so far away—Dolly had never been very good at understanding such things. *Attendez un moment,* said the operator at the hotel. Then: "Mrs. Jacobus, here's your call."

"Hello?" An unpleasant and familiar woman's voice sounded in Dolly's ears. For a second she failed to understand: why, it was the wooden voice of Esther, ugly, gum-chewing, wigged Esther. The secretary. Then she understood. Slowly she replaced the receiver.

The long-distance operator was persistent. She rang again. "Your call to Valletta, Mrs. Jacobus."

"I've changed my mind," Dolly said. "Please cancel it. I've changed my mind."

*S*o that's how it is, said Dolly out loud in the empty apartment. That's how it's been all the time. I've really always known. But what actors we all are.

She turned off the light and sat on the windowsill, looking out at the broad canopy of sky and many lights. Something fell away from her and dropped, perhaps the paths that henceforward would go their different ways,

with cosmic speed, so that there would be no remember-
ing even when she had still been her undivided self.

Why, one ought to, said Dolly out loud to the shad-
owy paintings, whose frames glittered silently in the
dark room. One ought to.

Tomorrow, she thought, I'll know what one ought to do.

Translated by Hillel Halkin

The Emissary

*H*e came in through the back door, weary and angry, even though I had opened the door before he rang. The truth is I had somehow expected him while drinking my coffee, in the vague knowledge that today it would happen again.

*H*e came in like smoke, gray, somewhat stifling, with an unpleasant smell. His remaining hair was yellowish, like parched, abandoned stalks. He sat down on the kitchen chair without leaving hold of his open briefcase, into which he directed his anger.

"Well?" he said impatiently.

"For whom is it today?" I asked, defending myself by making conversation.

He made a disparaging gesture with his hand. A piece of cigarette paper clung to his mouth.

"Orphans from the Sahara. Well, give, come on—give."

I turned slowly to the wardrobe and with submissive hands took out several pairs of shoes. I held them out to him with bowed head, though I had no idea what orphans from the Sahara could do with my high-heeled shoes, which were no longer mine and perhaps never had been, having been lent me for the one evening, for that walk hand-in-hand in the street, for those slightly intoxicated hours, when I was not responsible either for my words, which became impertinent, or my hands, which came to life in a kind of movement of their own, while the heels drummed and soared.

He spat on the floor.

I went back to the wardrobe and selected a dress that had a stain. He fingered the cloth and found the stain at once.

"You, too," he rebuked me. "Just like the rest."

"Perhaps the stain can be removed," I said. Unsmilingly he bared two rows of gray teeth. A profound weariness was reflected in his eyes, a sorrow intermittently replenished; he was like a boxer's old punching bag, still suffering blow after blow, still returning to the hand that struck it.

"A dress," he said bitterly, "a rag, a few threads, while there—do you want me to tell you about it?"

I felt the tears brimming in my eyes even before he began. A curse has afflicted me since birth—call it empathy; for that reason there are some dreadful expressions I pretend not to hear: words like *orphans, poverty, accident, bombs,* or *murder.* But that morning he was merciless. He wiped his forehead with open, dirty palm, and said:

"Nuclear tests last year. They are born without . . ."

I blocked my ears so as not to hear, not with my hands but by a kind of faculty I have developed to make myself completely deaf, and knelt down beside the wardrobe drawer, choking back my tears. Time and again when he returned—from Asia, the North Pole, Honolulu, Timbuktu, the jungles of Brazil—he would threaten me with his stories. And the terrible thing was that I guessed all of them, as if they came out of me. As if they were me.

I took out all my coats, and then added my stockings. He pushed me aside, went to the wardrobe and took out a striped, red and white skirt, which I used to wear only on mornings when I got up absolutely certain of triumph. I shared a secret with that skirt. It belonged entirely to me and I belonged entirely to it, in days of roaring light.

And now it was being pawed by the ugly, nail-bitten hands of the emissary.

"It's mine," I protested weakly, though I knew what his answer would be.

"Yours," he sneered and spat on the floor, "you-rs."

I asked forgiveness from all my gods for committing the sin of self-adornment, the sin of arrogance. For hadn't I known all the time, all the time, even when wearing it, that it was not mine—because nothing belongs to you in this world, not even your own body— and the exhilaration it used to arouse in me was but the sweetness of stolen waters, the joy of transgression, the pride of transient sin.

I wanted to give him the skirt myself, but before I could do so he had deposited it, crumpled, in his briefcase, leaving me choking on chagrin and pride.

The emissary paid no more attention to me. He

brusquely removed everything from the shelves—lingerie, cosmetics, all the contrivances of women, lurking in hiding, beckoning from the shelves, all the delusions of the great hope, all the little acts of creation compounding fantasy.

The wardrobe was not completely empty. He began pacing about the room, as though concluding a repulsive task, removed the roses from the vase and put them in his briefcase, stripped off the sheets, leafed quickly through the books and took the best ones.

"What's that?" he suddenly asked, his sad heartrending eyes contemplating the housecoat I was wearing.

"A housecoat," I answered, "there's nothing else left."

He sank into the chair and didn't even get angry, just covered his eyes with his hand.

"In other words," he said slowly, "you're just as rotten as the rest."

I wasn't rotten. I didn't want to be rotten, to dole out pittances, to give in exact measure, like half an oath, half a fast, a divided city, like a broker forever multiplying and dividing. I didn't know how to be rotten. A kind of latent truth is always lurking in the air around me, and only terrifying expressions like *orphans* or *nuclear tests* can make it materialize and illuminate it around me. They were born without, and I was quibbling over a housecoat.

I undressed. I took a large plastic bag, in which I had once bought all the fruits of the season, and put it on. The red drawstring dangled slackly down, like a wound from my throat to the lower part of my stomach, but the wound did not hurt. The summer sun warmed my arms through the thin plastic. The roses, which were once

mine, emitted perfume from the emissary's shabby briefcase. I was glad they had left me their memory.

He suddenly turned his head to the wall, leaned his
forehead on both clenched fists, and began to cry.

"If you knew," he said, "if you had seen what I saw
there. It's incredible, it's incredible that man can do that
to man—and to little children too."

I wanted to console him from the depths of my plastic, but I knew there was no consolation for him, that he
carried all those things in his heart, bitter and alien.

He went out weeping into the street, and I stood beside the window warming myself in the transparent bag.
It occurred to me that it resembled the bag of waters en-
closing the fetus; and perhaps that was how it should
be—it is always possible to be born.

The smell of monstrous pity remained in the empty
room.

Translated by David Weber

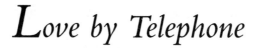

Love by Telephone

"*Ach,* Sergeant Fijoya! *Ach,* Sergeant Fijoya!"

*T*hey clap hands in distress, so seemingly helpless, self-defined at this complicated moment in timeless feminine terms of high heels and black lace petticoats, in which there is no possible way of crossing the terrible street called Afternoon, called A Sergeant From The Police Department sitting in their easy chair, right here in their own home, who could believe it? *Ach,* Sergeant Fijoya. If only he would scoop them up with his large palms, Eva in his left hand and Monika in his right, and cross them over safely himself. In their tailored Chanel suits. The *Modedamen.*

Sergeant Fijoya tries not to let all the *ach-ach*-ing distract him. This is the fifth day he has paid a call to this porcelainy, antimacassary, slipcovery house in which even the walls seem knit in pink wool. Why, for the love of God, would a sane person want to put a knitted slip-cover on a toilet seat? At times he finds himself lifting a large palm to ward off something in the air. Strange things that he can't put a finger on grow in this house. But the coffee is good. And the cakes. These last five days have taught him to appreciate the hidden power of a Meissen china cup. When he asked the first time if it were Israeli-made, they not unkindly laughed a tinkling little laugh that seemed to come from a music box. Sergeant Fijoya sits bulkily in his chair and sips coffee, warding off the unfathomable, getting a grip on the case.

For several weeks they have been getting crank telephone calls. Who would think it of two old women like them? The crank uses the foulest language. Each man shall die for his sin. Each man shall die for his sin. The sin of the unseen caller is immense, it is purple and infected, it stinks like a rotten eggplant. A disease in the midst of their house. All the obscene maleness that they have managed to keep from their door—fat cigars in the bathroom, belches, bills in oily leather wallets—has suddenly overrun them with these telephone calls. He deserves to die. If only Sergeant Fijoya would kill him, before their very eyes, via the telephone. He has a right to, he's a policeman. It's his job to clean up the world. Sergeant Fijoya may be a man, but his smell is a very delicate one, just a vaguely peanut-flavored scent. The police keep their uniforms clean.

"If it doesn't stop," says Monika, "we'll have to move out. This apartment is contaminated already."

"We will not move out," says Eva. "We will get rid of this nuisance. Won't we, Sergeant Fijoya?"

"Of course we will," says Sergeant Fijoya for the tenth time. "But tell me what he sounds like." He can't get an exact description from them.

"Like a sports announcer," says Eva despairingly in her bronchitic voice. "Only not so fast."

"Lady," Sergeant Fijoya reproves her, "what you're giving me isn't a description. It's an imaginary account."

Sergeant Fijoya's father had two wives, who lived in adjoining houses. Nicely built homes they were too, because the old man built them himself when he wasn't busy talking with God in the barn. Once, late at night, an Arab had knocked on the door. He cried and cried. Through the door, through the night, he confessed to old Fijoya that a year before he had cheated him out of a sack of hay, and ever since he and his family had been cursed. They hadn't had a day of good luck all year. Now, through the night, he asked Fijoya to forgive him. Fijoya forgave. He didn't open the door. Without moving he listened to the crying voice go away. His children watched him from under the blankets and promised themselves to build him an altar one day and sacrifice to him upon it. If he didn't ascend to heaven in a chariot before then, God forbid, or create some special world for himself to go live in.

These days, however, houses are different; you never know what you're getting into. In their knit home the two women regard him with angelic cunning from behind invisible fans. Old women like them should be in a protected place, surrounded by children and grandchildren. Something isn't clear, it isn't clear at all. His first time in this house he heard a screech in the corner and swung swiftly around, his hand on his pistol butt. But it was only a parrot, a large tropical bird named Vigor. Who ever heard of a parrot named Vigor? There was something insulting about it — not that they meant it as an insult, but there you were. Creepy. Like yesterday, when Monika invited him to stay for lunch and Eva went to look in the refrigerator. The two women consulted and told him there was *Kalb,* which means veal in German, but which he took to be Arabic, in which it means dog. It gave him the shivers.

"Recently, this annoyance, after midnight as well, imagine, Sergeant Fijoya, waking up at night for that."

"Does he call at regular times?"

"There's nothing regular about him. Sometimes he says a single word and hangs up."

"There are many perverts," says Sergeant Fijoya. "Uses filthy language a lot, does he?"

They flap their palms diminutively like frightened birds, as if to drive the crank away, not to have to talk about him, ugh, ugh.

Sergeant Fijoya has barely risen to go when the telephone rings. Monika looks at Eva. Eva looks at Monika.

"Answer the telephone, lady," says the sergeant, swinging into action. "Just say hello, and if it's him, pass the receiver to me."

Eva stands by the telephone, her dress trembling from the pounding of her heart. Sergeant Fijoya looms large, not that he's so big, there are bigger men than he, but right now he seems very big by her side. She utters a frail hello and immediately passes him the receiver, dropping it into his hand as though it were a bug.

Sergeant Fijoya listens for a few seconds and makes a disgusted face. "This is the police talking," he says. "You better shut your dirty trap, because we're on to you, you pervert. You'll be tried according to Article—"

But the crank hangs up without waiting for the number of the article. Sergeant Fijoya waits another moment with action-packed eyes, then hangs up too. They expect a miracle from him. If the police can't make miracles, who can?

"Who is it, Sergeant Fijoya? Do you know him? Did you recognize his voice? Do you have a file on him?"

He stands there thoughtfully, saying nothing. Finally he declares:

"He's not an ordinary crank. When an ordinary crank hears police, he panics. This one didn't panic. He's a mean one."

"A mean one," they echo, their arms falling. Such sad words.

"Never mind," says Fijoya. "We'll catch him. We have ways." He takes out a pad and jots something down. "I'm going to the telephone company now. If your connection on the phone suddenly goes bad, don't worry, it just means we're listening in. But from now on I'll need your full cooperation."

"Of course," they reply, overflowing with anxiety, "of course."

"What I mean is, we'll have to catch him together. If he calls, you mustn't throw the phone down right away like Madam Eva did before. On the contrary, you have to keep him talking for a long, long time. Long enough for the telephone people to trace the number he's calling from, so that we can get there and nab him in the act. Do you get me?"

"Of course," they reply, very unhappily. "Of course."

Fijoya knows that it won't be easy for them to keep the crank talking a long, long time. As he looks at them, in fact, he knows that it's impossible. But there is nothing else to say.

"It's the only way," he declares as he leaves. He has a nice walk, there is music somewhere in his shoulders. They hear his car driving off, and with it, their only salvation.

"We didn't even invite him for coffee," says Monika sadly.

"He wouldn't have stayed. He has too much to do."

"He has too much to do," agrees Monika. "But they'll listen."

"Yes."

The two of them sit in their easy chairs, staring at the telephone, their aged hands folded in their laps.

"Stop staring at that telephone all day!" Tiberius Kovacs's voice resounds in the room. His violin case in one hand, he is on his way to the weekly concert at the YMCA auditorium. The violinist Tiberius Kovacs is a gigantic, black, bespectacled heron whose gothic movements send arches of stained glass flying high in all directions. Another thing about him is that he is living his life in reverse. When the Nazis came to Hungary, Tibor Kovacs was a very old man of nine. Now he is a child and getting younger every year. He goes over to Vigor's cage.

"Vigor! Vigor!"

The parrot cackles lispingly in protest.

"I'm going to eat you," Tiberius promises. "You'll be parrot-*au-feu*. You'll be parrot *Tiberiade*. Parrot Kovacs. Tonight."

"Tiberius, really," Monika admonishes.

But Eva says, "Why dream about parrots when we have a marvelous soup? Put that horrid violin of yours in the corner and sit down like a human being."

"A-hh-h," growls Tiberius happily. "I'll look in the refrigerator. I'll peek in the pots. I'll open all the doors."

"You know it's not permitted," says Eva, lighting a cigarette. "You'll sit and wait patiently."

"I'll peek under your skirts," says Tiberius in a terrible whisper.

"How boring you are, Tiberius. What are you playing this evening?"

Tiberius makes a face. "Ugh. Liszt. Grieg. Rachmaninoff. A program for virgins of both sexes. And what a conductor. The deafest, dumbest, and densest we've had all year. During the rehearsal yesterday, in the middle of the Grieg, I played him four bars of 'Ach, du lieber Augustin.' He's so deaf he couldn't even hear it. Blanker than a wall. Tonight I'm going to do it again."

"You wouldn't dare. During the concert?"

"I'll dare all right. You'll hear it on the radio. It'll be toward the end of the first movement of the Grieg."

Tiberius begins to sing the score, but they look suspiciously at the telephone.

"Stop looking at that telephone all day!" he shouts again.

From the kitchen Monika adds, "You know, he's never called during a concert."

*I*n the little kitchen, or rather kitchenette, stands a small refrigerator covered with an embroidered napkin. Monika spins back and forth like a top from the refrigerator to the sink, from the sink to the stove, always in the same orbit: Monika—Akinom—Monika—Akinom. The space she occupies within the confines of the room is measured, precise, crystalline, well-lit. In the street she is a picture, she and Eva, the *Modedamen,* both cut from the fashion pages. They sew their own clothes with fabric ordered from England and have been the pride of the neighborhood for the past forty years. Monika has never married. Eva, who once was, arrived from Germany with a disappointing daughter named Steffi. Mother and daughter hated each other for several years, until Steffi grew up and left Israel. Monika and Eva were left by themselves, twin queens of the street, down which they strolled with slow regality like carnival dolls, smiling at everyone without seeing who anyone was. What shoes, what hairstyles. They were the first to wear midis, the first to wear long sleeves with short sleeves over them. Not mere colors. It's no trick to dress colorfully, any teenager can do it; in fact, Eva says that color is the aesthetic of the masses. No, what we are talking about is a sense of taste that is authoritative, almost divine. It is Eva and Monika who bring us the seasons of the year, in and out. When the *Modedamen* put on their tweed skirts, autumn has really arrived and all our worthless summer dresses turn into rags that must be put away for the year. And spring? The *Modedamen* proclaim it ambassadorially by appearing for the first time in their flowery dresses, marching slowly down the street as though leading a parade: now it is official.

Little Monika asks Eva, who is taller than she, to get

the *Teufel*-pan down from the shelf. The *Teufel*-pan is the
Teflon pan, but Monika has no gift for such complicated
words. Sometimes Eva teases her: "Monika, what's that
word . . . come on, what kind of meditation is it?"

"What?" asks Monika, alarmed, struggling to con-
centrate.

"Come on, Monika. Trans . . . trans–something meditation. What is it?"

"Transistorial!" beams Monika triumphantly. She
beams so broadly with each mistake that one can't possibly be cross with her. Eva gave up being cross long ago,
and now only smiles.

*M*onika's *Teufel*-pan is already sputtering on the stove, as
though there were a devil in it. Tiberius stretches out his
legs in the easy chair and complains:

"Why do I have to play tonight? Why? What suffering!"

"Because you get paid for it," says Eva, setting the
table.

"I have a split personality," says Tiberius darkly.

"Stop talking nonsense," says Eva. "You don't have
enough personality to split."

But he isn't listening. He has taken a cube of sugar
from the table and is sucking it intently. He is always
sucking sweets. His pockets are full of candies. He sucks
them during concerts too. The *Modedamen* regard this
habit disapprovingly.

*T*iberius is already young enough to be the son of either
of them. Perhaps he will be, too, when he reaches infancy

in a few more years. The two women haven't changed for twenty or thirty years: it's as though they were embalmed. The same Monika and the same Eva, just a little tougher and less supple, like old rubber. They will never die, they will one day simply crumble away like a wedding cake that has been standing for several decades in the baker's window. They have always gone to concerts together, wonderfully dressed; but it is winter now and easier to listen to the radio at home. Tiberius visits often, gathering in the folds of his coat, like a heron landing. He assists them with their tax returns and helps them find lost sums in their checkbooks. Monika is always losing sums. She forgets to write her checks down.

"*Kvatsch!* That woman shouldn't be allowed to hold a checkbook in her hands!" shouts Tiberius each time. Monika always smiles and serves him more soup. Electric bills, municipal taxes—it's all so complicated. Tiberius conjures figures, counting in Hungarian.

The three of them sit down at the table to eat the excellent soup. They tell him about Fijoya. He had promised to listen.

"They won't find a thing," says Tiberius impatiently. "They won't find anyone. There simply isn't any such person."

"What do you mean?"

"It's all coming from your own subconscious."

"But Tiberius, we've heard him. Fijoya heard him too."

"Naturally," says Tiberius victoriously. "You've created him."

"Tiberius, you're talking nonsense again."

"I am not talking nonsense. Why don't I ever get calls

like that? Because there's nothing the matter with my subconscious."

"Your subconscious is revolting," says Monika. "I don't know why we keep on feeding you."

"Because my wife can't cook." His voice grows ingratiating. "How many times have I said to her, 'Rojy, if this doesn't work' "—he pats his hollow stomach— " 'then this doesn't either.' She doesn't get it."

"Your Rojy," says Eva, "is an angel. I don't know of another woman who would put up with your turning on the shortwave to hear concerts at three o'clock in the morning."

"And with your screaming, every time you hear a mistake."

"Rojy," says Tiberius with a mixture of disdain and annoyance, "never wakes up."

"How do you know?"

Tiberius starts to answer, but the telephone rings. The two women freeze with their soup spoons halfway to their mouths. Tiberius goes to the telephone.

"Hello? Yes. Yes. Fine, I'll tell them." He turns to Eva and Monika. "It's the telephone company. They say that from now on they'll be listening in on the line. And that you should try to keep the conversation going as long as possible."

Thank God at least for that.

The two women relax. Little by little, with difficulty, but visibly enough, order is being restored to the world. The starlings outside the window swirl in spirals, like flakes of soot above a campfire, windblown, catching a last ray of red light. Winter is here. The telephone people are listening. They'll catch him, no doubt of it. The rainy season, too, will begin on time.

Tiberius stretches. "That hits the spot. I'm ready for anything now, even Grieg."

He puts on his black coat. At the door he turns and yells: "So, my lovelies, there's no such person at all. He's simply a figment of your subconscious. Trust Tiberius."

*I*n the apartment next door, Mrs. Carasso, buckled, manicured, and packaged, looks out through her peephole. She doesn't like all these policemen snooping around. The Carassos moved in two years ago, they paid a lot of money for this place, and now, police. This isn't what they moved for. That man saying good-bye now was no policeman, but perhaps he was a secret agent carrying a violin case for disguise. With two such old ladies, not even married, who can know? Mrs. Carasso would very much like it if both would disappear. Her children are growing up and she has her eyes on their apartment. In a few more years she can join it to her own to make a proper house. The two old ladies can't live forever. Mrs. Carasso is biding her time. And meanwhile there are plans. Once she dropped in on her neighbors, supposedly to borrow half a lemon, and managed to plan the whole apartment. Which sideboard would go where. Out of the corner of her eye.

*T*hat evening, toward the end of the first movement of the Grieg, Eva and Monika bend close to the radio. Amid a tangle of violins the strains of "Ach, du lieber Augustin, Augustin, Augustin" sound with thin impudence. They look at each other in shock.

"No!"

"He did it!"

"He'll be thrown out of the orchestra one day," says Eva, uncertain whether to laugh or be afraid. Her chin quivers.

"*Ach,* Tiberius. What a fellow. *Ach, du lieber.*"

*I*t is Monika's secret vice that she changes her bedclothes every day. She cannot climb into a bed that has even one single shadow of a crease. Her greatest pleasure is to re-move the bedspread every evening and catch sight of the snow-white pillow and the unsullied sheets that have come straight from the laundry. Each sleep is a new ex-perience, one she has never had before. Monika doesn't just love cleanliness, Monika is cleanliness itself. Purity is recreated nightly in her bed.

"A dirty young person," says Monika, "can still be charming, but God protect us from a dirty old one."

Hence her fragrant baths three times a day. And the pleasure of climbing into her own special bed.

A pleasure-molded voice: "Eva?"

"What?"

"Which is younger, Jerusalem or the Dead Sea?"

Eva smiles a long, long smile and puts out her ciga-rette. "Why?"

"Because the Dead Sea seems younger to me," says Monika.

"Jerusalem is the Dead Sea's grandmother. Now go to sleep."

"Jerusalem is everybody's grandmother."

Silence. Then once more: "Eva."

"What?"

"Do you want to know something about Fijoya?"

"He's nice. What else?"

"He has a smile like a watermelon. You're smoking in bed again, Eva. I can smell it from here."

"I'm already too old to die young," says Eva coarsely, turning off her light. She knows she has broken the rules: death is not a permissible subject in this house. Monika is audibly insulted.

"Good-night, Monika."

No answer.

At three-thirty in the morning the telephone rings. Monika calls from the cavern of her room: "Eva, answer it."

"You answer it."

"I can't."

Silence. The telephone goes on ringing. It must have awakened the whole building by now. Mrs. Carasso in the morning, a predictable sourness.

"Well," says Eva from the darkness of her room, "one really can't be expected to answer at night. The man listening at the telephone company must have gone to bed already. All those obscenities will just go to waste."

The telephone rings a few more times and stops. The whole house continues to vibrate.

"Big heroine," says Monika quietly under her blanket.

*I*n the brilliant morning the starlings soar high. Eva notices with a hidden smile that Monika has failed to dust the telephone. She is too scared to touch it. Eva picks up a dust rag, and the telephone rings beneath it. She springs to the other end of the room as though a bomb has gone off in her hand. It is only Fijoya.

"Madam Eva? Is everything all right?"

"Y . . . yes." Nothing in the world can make her admit that they didn't answer the telephone last night.

"I just wanted you to know that I'm on duty today. If anything comes up, I'll be right over. The important thing is to keep the pervert talking. Don't be afraid of him, he's harmless. We'll catch him, don't worry."

In the police station Officer Avitan says to Fijoya, "I see you're on a big case."

Sergeant Fijoya looks at him coldly. "You, Avitan, may have gone through ten courses in police school, but no course ever went through you."

Avitan stands his ground. "What danger!"

At that very moment Monika is saying to Eva, "Eva, let's go somewhere. Let's take a vacation at the Dead Sea. For a week or two. By then it will have stopped by itself."

"That's cowardice," says Eva. "Besides which, who will water the flowerpots?"

"Mrs. Carasso."

A grimace. "Everything she touches dies. Last year I gave her a dianthus and it died. Just look at her geranium. It takes real talent to kill a geranium. But I'll tell you what: we'll go to the Dead Sea as soon as they catch him. Then we'll treat ourselves to a trip."

A sudden, strong-hued vision floods the eyeballs: shocking blue amid sun-bronzed masses of rock, violet browns, an asphalt sea road. A soughing of reeds. A happiness of palms. Jerusalem suddenly seems wintry and decrepit, full of stone wreckages.

"Is that a promise?" asks Monika.

"It's a promise. But first let's finish this business."

Eva puts on her little bonnet to go out. Monika says, "Buy some black thread for the sewing machine."

"I will. And Monika, answer the phone. None of your tricks now, Monika."

"All right. Just come back soon."

*E*va leaves. She returns. A minute later she rings the Carassos' doorbell. The Carassos' son, a soldier on leave from his commando unit, opens the door.

"It's Monika," says Eva. "In the bathroom. On the floor. She's wet. She's dead."

They run to her. So small and pitiful, small-boned like a crinkled bird. The crinkled things of this world. Fledglings, old people, flower buds.

Eva trembles all over but speaks clearly, as though she sees it all perfectly.

"The telephone must have rung. That's what happened. The telephone rang and scared her. She wanted to run. A heart attack. Maybe before she fell, maybe after. No, it's pointless to call a doctor. You can see for yourself."

"Yes," says young Carasso uncertainly. He has seen dead young men on the battlefield, but never a dead, naked old lady. The sight of her shocks him. And in the bath yet. "Come, let's cover her," he says to Eva. Something is missing here, perhaps a dogtag.

*T*hey cover Monika. A crowd begins to form, congregating in the stairway. Officer Avitan elbows his way through it. Children throng near the police car, eager to see how the flashing light works. There is no one to show them.

Eva sits in the easy chair, her back very straight, and says: "She was frightened because she was naked. The phone ringing when she was naked, that's what did it. And all by herself in the house. Maybe it was the crank. If only she'd had a slip on. If only she'd managed to put one on first. This way . . . it's awfully cruel when a person is naked. She's defenseless. No thanks, no coffee for me. You're all terribly kind. I'll take a pill and I'll be fine. Thank you all. It's only because she was naked."

The bathroom is redolent of Yardley's Lavender. "Do you need all this water?" young Carasso asks Officer Avitan.

Avitan bends over, sticks in a hand, and pulls out the plug. The scented water drains slowly out of the bath, gurgles and whirls, and departs with a long, long sigh of finality. Standing in the doorway Mrs. Carasso remarks out of the corner of her eye that the plumbing must be checked before the children move in. The smell of lavender dissipates slowly and disappears.

*M*onika is buried on a day of rain-swollen mountains. The starlings form blurred, crooked lines on the wires and TV aerials, like letters on page proofs with many nervous mistakes. The world is all smeary. Eva is an abdicated queen. You can't be a single *Modedame,* by yourself, they must come in pairs. The coat she is wearing seems to belong to someone else, it is terribly old and there is very little Eva inside it. Tiberius's face falls away from itself, a double image. Every now and then he pulls out a handkerchief and tries patting it back into place.

Monika is covered with earth. The rain falls harder. *Finis.*

Eva pauses by a wet pine and says to Tiberius: "Tiberius, is it true? What I think?"

He nods miserably. His face is wet.

"Why?"

"It was a k-k-kind of joke. An unsuccessful one."

Eva shakes her head heavily. She is really old now. "It wasn't our subconscious," she says. "It was yours."

"I want to die," bleats Tiberius.

Fijoya stands on the path above without coming down to the grave. He prefers to avoid the congestion.

"Madam Eva, I'm terribly sorry. Really, from the bottom of my heart. If you need any help . . . "

Eva lays a soft hand on Fijoya's sleeve. Her other hand grips Tiberius's arm, as though binding them in a secret alliance.

"Sergeant Fijoya, this is our friend Mr. Kovacs, from the orchestra. He . . . "

But suddenly she fears that Sergeant Fijoya will punish him for the "Ach, du lieber Augustin." Perhaps it's better not to introduce them. Life is so difficult. A man meets a police sergeant, and the next thing you know he's exposed and thrown out of the orchestra. She turns pale. Fijoya helps her sit on a rock.

"You'll visit Madam Eva," he orders Tiberius.

"I will. Every day."

"Every day," says Fijoya, looking at him sharply.

This, then, is his sentence.

Translated by Hillel Halkin

My Straw Chairs

Just then many shallow and frivolous people had begun to dabble in literature, which pained me considerably. Perhaps that was what got me into the predicament I'm in. Why should I care about literature, you ask, I who am a lonely woman about to retire from my job as a book-keeper for the Sick Fund? After all, I deal with numbers, not authors. But I do like to go to lectures, of which Jerusalem has no end. All this because I love literature — and not sentimentally either, the way amateurs do, because I'm a harsh critic and not your emotional type. I'm not one of your high school girls who discovers boys and poetry all in one week.

What I wanted to say was that lately all sorts of poseurs have been permitted not only to publish but even to lecture in public. Often I sit through some talk and I suffer, actually suffer, so that I go home feeling personally insulted. I'm sure I must have been feeling that

way the day I brought my straw chairs to be fixed, because otherwise what happened would not have. And
what happened was this.

Since the wicker chairs in my kitchen had dried out from
many days of desert heat, and the straw was beginning to
snap, I brought them for repairs to a man in a dark little
den of a workshop on one of those narrow Jerusalem al-
leys where electric drills and saws whine all day. How
people can even work in such places without shutting
their ears is beyond me. The cart driver who brought my
chairs put them down in the middle of the vaulted alley,
took his fare, and left. It grieved me to see them standing
like unwanted guests: in my kitchen they were handsome to look at; here in the street they resembled penni-
less beggars. The repairman took them disparagingly
and tossed them into a corner with some other destitute
furniture, between a rocking chair whose belly had burst
and a large chest filled with rags. In two or three weeks,
he said. Better yet, come back in a month. It was so dark
in his shop that I could barely make out his face. I didn't
know why it took so long to do such relatively simple
work, but he told me with obvious displeasure that he
didn't attend to such things himself — meaning, of course,
to cheap chairs like my own. He gave them to a group
of old people, who worked on them slowly, more as a
hobby than a job. When I inquired why I couldn't save
time by bringing the chairs directly to the old people
myself, he replied that their address was confidential.
Suddenly he flew into a rage. Lifting one of my chairs
with a menacing hand, he said:

"Listen, lady, I don't need them, you can take them

back if you want. They're nothing but trouble for me—trouble with the old people, trouble with the customers, trouble with the income tax. A person tries to do a favor and this is what he gets."

I stared at the floor and said nothing, since there was no one else around who would take my chairs at all. He turned a cross and burly shoulder to me, and said:

"All right, then. Give your name to the woman over there, and pay her something in advance."

Only now did I notice the squat woman sitting in a corner of the shop behind an ancient, paper-piled counter that might have been a century old. Real junk it was, though good enough perhaps for the accounts of a workshop like this. The woman behind it was staring at me, staring, I could see, with bold, disconcerting eyes. For the life of me I couldn't understand why there was so much hostility in this place. She told me how much to pay and I asked if I could pay her by check.

"What's your address?" she snapped.

Why, I'll never know, perhaps because of her curt tone, perhaps because I was still thinking of last evening's lecture, which had annoyed me greatly, having been given by a fraud, I replied:

"Authors House."

"Ah," said the woman. "So you're an author."

To this day I don't know why I nodded that I was. I could blush for shame when I think of it. But facts are facts, and, know why or not, that's what I did. There are lies that a person will tell in a dark, noisy shop that she never would tell in broad daylight where people can see. To make matters worse, I don't even like the word *author,* which seems less a title that authors take for themselves than one appropriated by critics, professors, fraudulent lecturers, and all the others who spend their time on the noisy periphery of the small, still voice. At most, it seems to me, a person is an author only at the moment that he actually writes and ceases to be one as soon as he stops. You can call him a pedestrian then, or an eater, or a sewer-on-of-buttons-on-his-coat, but certainly not an author. I swear I don't know what got into me then.

The woman rose slightly from her seat and pointed a hand at me, extending her fat little arm to its full length:

"So what are you writing about me for? Who gave you permission to take people's lives and write them up?"

Her shouting frightened me. Years ago, before I was a bookkeeper for the Sick Fund, I worked as a receptionist in the clinic. Because there were always bullying patients shouting at me, and I couldn't stand their anger, I became very ill and had to be transferred to the accounting department. These days you can never be sure that you know all there is to know about yourself. Everybody in the street knows more than you do. Psychologists, statisticians, journalists. If someone stands up and accuses you, there's no saying you aren't guilty. And even if you aren't, your subconscious is.

"But I don't even know you," I tried saying. This just made her shout even louder.

"That has nothing to do with it. You authors know everything. Bad people tell you things, people with big mouths, and you listen and write it all down and get rich. You live off our miseries. I hope you all burn."

I asked her what story and whose life she had in mind. She began to laugh.

"Just look at her playing the innocent. Butter wouldn't melt in her mouth."

"But I don't know what you're talking about."

"Of course you do," she declared, leering at me meanly.

She sat down again, very stout, her eyes glittering triumphantly in the darkness like black patent-leather buttons. All this while the repairman stood looking off into another corner with his back to us, though he was clearly not unaware of what was happening. Two people can sit at opposite ends of a room and still talk to each other with their bodies, even with hidden love. Yet the language spoken here was the language of war. Of ancient, backbiting hostility.

I left. Strong sunlight streamed through an opening in the vaulted archway outside the shop. Where it fell on the sidewalk stood a young man in a gray undershirt who was smoothing a large board on a hand-lathe. Chips of wood shot off in all directions, gleaming like gold sparks as they flew into the dark alley. Sparks that did not hurt, for the young man failed to flinch when several fell upon his shoulder.

"Excuse me," I said to him. "There's something I'd like to ask you."

He stopped and frowned at me for interrupting his work. I was no longer so sure that I wanted to ask the question, but since I had already intruded, I said:

"Tell me, isn't there something strange about that woman at the counter in there?"

The minute I asked I felt sorry. What did I know about it, perhaps the young man was the woman's son, and here I was opening my mouth. But he answered me tranquilly enough:

"There's nothing strange about her."

He paused and repeated:

"There's nothing strange about *that* woman."

He returned to his lathe.

I regretted having bothered him, a young working-man like him, where would the world be if not for a man who works with his hands? This wasn't my lucky alley, and so I hurried to leave it, skipping over piles of wooden chips lying between light and shade, over wrenches and heavy doorlatches. I turned into another roofed alley in which lay torn sacks of wormy vegetables from the nearby marketplace and finally reemerged into sunlit streets and the sights I knew well.

*W*ithout its chairs my kitchen was strangely empty, yet it was still mine. I knew every inch of it. I noticed that where one of the chairs had stood some paint had peeled and left a crack on the exposed wall. Well, I'm a scrubber. I like things to be orderly and neat. I took a small paint-brush and a can of putty such as I always keep handy and retouched the wall, smoothed it out, and painted it over. The kitchen was spic-and-span. I didn't feel up to a lecture, who knows what a person will encounter once he leaves his own house, the surprises there are in this world — sometimes I have the strength for them and sometimes I don't, so toward evening I went out for a walk, as I do on lectureless days. In the street I met Theo Stein, who was out walking too. We stood by Government Place, where the ravens flock.

Jerusalem is full of ravens. Theo Stein used to say that they were reincarnations of the soldiers of the Tenth Roman Legion that captured Jerusalem after the long siege. They looted and stole so much, he said, that they lost their soldierly bearing. The proof of it was that no one ever saw a dead raven. Dead sparrows, yes, run-over pigeons, yes, dead thrushes fallen from their nests, yes, but never a dead raven. He talked Latin to them and claimed they understood him perfectly, although they acted clever and tried to conceal it. Nevertheless, they gathered wherever he walked, their raucous voices dry and mocking, like self-important beggars or perhaps like an old group of emigrants that will never return, whether in the woods of Augusta Victoria by the road leading off into the desert, or by Government Place. Large, gray-black, hoppity birds whose every hop was a little hill in the air, connoisseurs of the city's conspicuous stones. Last, decrepit Romans.

In recent years Theo Stein has taken his evening walk by himself, without his wife. I like Theo Stein, like to see him walking in the distance in his short pants with the broad stride of an elderly athlete, a small rucksack slung over one shoulder as though it were a map case, his glasses and knees reddening in the great swath of sunset light. Until several years ago he walked with his wife, a woman with a wonderfully beautiful face and hair clipped short like a boy's. One never got used to the contrast between her boyish head and her bloated body, which defied all attempts at demarcation as though it were a blob of liquid held in by her dress. It was all the fault of the tranquilizers that she took day and night on orders from the doctors and that were practically her only food. Since a cure was impossible, the next best thing was to sedate her — although if you ask me, all these sedatives simply mean that the doctors have failed. When

Theo Stein walked with Lotte, he didn't stride like an athlete or carry a rucksack; he walked slowly, supporting her weight, as though fearful of spilling her. Toward evening, when the heat fades and the air is blessedly refreshing, Jerusalem is full of old couples out for a walk. Sometimes I don't know what I've done to deserve to live in Jerusalem. The city gives so much of itself, so much, cool breezes and lovely sunsets and lately even municipal gardeners who work hard and plant lovely things for us. Once I saw the Steins walking when a truck suddenly cut in front of them on Saadia Ga'on Street. It was not a particularly unusual occurrence in this age of reckless driving—who isn't startled at least a few times a day by such a truck roaring by? Yet Lotte Stein's panic was out of all proportion, there was something not sane about it. "Theo, Theo," she started to cry in a high-pitched howl, until he seized her shoulders like a vise and shouted, "Quiet, I want quiet right now!" They continued on their way, he scolding her roundly while she cried.

Since her illness Lotte stopped saying hello to me. In recent years, however, she hasn't gone out at all, so that I only run into Theo, who always stops to chat a bit with me. Even if we are both out walking, we never walk side by side. We just stand in one place for a while, which is no accident, because generally people who walk together are couples, but Theo Stein and I are not a couple, we are just two people who happened to have met in the street. There is a tactfulness between Theo Stein and me. We stop to chat but do not walk together.

Lotte Stein has been repeatedly hospitalized, released, and rehospitalized, and Theo has had time for walking only when she is put away. When she is home he has to take care of her, to cook and resew her dresses, which are always bursting at the seams because of her drugged awkwardness and swollen limbs, so that he gets out at most for a quarter of an hour in the evening to stretch his legs a bit. When he leaves he carefully locks the door and makes sure to disconnect the telephone and the doorbell with a small screwdriver that he always keeps in his pocket, so that his wife is protected from all contact with strangers. A strange voice, a strange face can frighten her to tears, so that not even all the drugs in the house can calm her. Sometimes he has had to return her to the hospital in the middle of a vacation. Such things have happened more than once.

They say that Lotte Stein already needed treatment as a high school student. She was nineteen when she arrived from Europe and still hadn't finished high school—in fact, there was nothing she could start and finish properly—and it was pointless for her to sit with sixteen- and seventeen-year-olds who were abler and nimbler than she. Perhaps she shouldn't have married either. Yet Theo Stein was determined; she was unhappy in school; and her family seized at the straw. Instead of improving, however, she only deteriorated. Two or three years after her illness had been officially diagnosed, and declared to be incurable, there was an incident with a plumber who had been working in several apartments of the building. He was a laconic, curly-headed young man who wore old army fatigues to work and had no idea that Lotte had fallen in love with him—indeed, that she was bent on a courtly, European-style romance with bouquets of flowers and tender love letters. Who is to say that she didn't deserve one? In those days she wasn't yet bloated from the drugs, there was just a wild cunning in her eyes. But the plumber noticed nothing and may never have looked in her eyes; if her immediate and total surrender from the moment he entered her kitchen surprised him, he let it go at that. He finished changing the fittings in all eight apartments of the building and—being a skilled worker whose services were much in demand—went off to other jobs.

*F*rom then on Lotte Stein took a turn for the worse. She still more or less functioned as a housewife—sometimes more and sometimes less, so that Theo Stein never knew if he would find a meal waiting for him when he came home from work—but even on days when she functioned she set the table for three, for, as she explained to Theo, the plumber was apt to return any moment and she wanted the house to be ready for him, since they were lovers and were going to elope. Afterward, when she stopped functioning entirely, Theo obediently went on setting the table for three, because he didn't want to upset her. Until one day he felt that he had had enough and told Lotte's doctor that he wasn't setting three places anymore even if all the psychiatrists in the world should counsel him otherwise. He had taken as much as he could.

I don't know what the doctor said to Lotte. Perhaps he told her that the plumber had gone off to America, perhaps he was drafted by the army. Unfortunately there are times when one has to resort to deception, though both the world and the deceiver are diminished in the process. At any rate, from now on Lotte agreed to a table set for two, just for her and Theo, only occasionally reminding him, as though some signal had flashed in her brain: "Yes, yes, but next week we'll need three place settings again, won't we, Theo?" And Theo would grit his teeth and say, "Perhaps, we'll have to see."

This too was a temporary phase. Eventually Lotte Stein took to sleeping most of the time. When she didn't sleep, she ate sweets. The door had to be locked at all times.

*F*or a while Theo refused to accept the situation and fought back. His gestures in those days were those of a man who is chasing off flies, or water from a relentless sprinkler that pursues him wherever he goes. I know a fair amount about what went on in their house at this time, because Theo Stein came to visit me now and then. Sometimes, agitated, he would tell me about things that happened in plain words, but more often it would be indirectly. It wasn't easy for him. He would sit there on tenterhooks. Once he even bent the prongs of a cake fork out of shape, one by one, without noticing it, so that I had to bring it in to a shop near the market to be fixed. And once he said:

"This generation thinks that it invented sex. Its mothers and grandmothers did more and talked less. I'll tell you what a woman used to do when her lover left her. She went to her wash basin and scrubbed and beat all day, all day long on the washboard until her hands were raw. By evening the wash was done, there was a meal on the table, and nobody could guess that anything was wrong, not her husband and certainly not her children. Today everyone has a washing machine or a laundry, there's nothing to beat, so they all run to psychiatrists."

I served him good coffee. You won't find any of your instant coffee or tea bags in my house. Tea is tea with me and coffee is coffee. He sipped it avidly and said:

"Blessed be the coffeemakers of this world."

He thanked me and left.

So you see, years ago Theo Stein used to visit, and if he stopped coming, this was only because of an embarrassment between us. The fact of the matter is that a woman I worked with at the Sick Fund had already suggested to me that Theo Stein would be a good "solution" for me, which hurt my feelings a great deal. What did I need a solution for if I didn't have a problem? And then, in that period of his life when Theo was still resisting his fate, thrashing about like a swimmer in a whirlpool who creates more whirlpools with every stroke, he came to me one Saturday afternoon and halfheartedly propositioned me, pessimistic in advance about the outcome. I declined in no uncertain terms. He himself, so it seemed, hadn't expected anything else. Since then we have retained our twilight-time friendship, but only in the street, no longer in my house. As I've said, there is a tactfulness between Theo Stein and me.

It took me a few days to get over this incident. His proposal offended me. It was like the time the thieves broke into the Sick Fund office at night, though everyone knows that I keep only accounts at my desk, and certainly no money or anything else worth taking. Still, they searched everywhere and made a mess of the room.

The sight of it in the morning made me physically ill, because I'm such an orderly woman, and here was everything upside-down. It was the same with Theo Stein. I
hope I'll be forgiven for saying so, but I, who am a
woman of nearly fifty on the verge of retirement, have
always looked for a certain beauty in people, and there
is nothing beautiful about Theo Stein. Nothing at all.
Perhaps I should explain what sort of beauty I mean. The
beauty I look for in a man should be like the beauty of
this country in which I live—this country that I love
with an undivided love, it is all that I have. What I miss
in people is a kind of starkness; there is so much su-
perfluity about them. Theo Stein is too articulate, too
cultured, if I may say so, too foreign in his speech. And
the way he gesticulates. And all his apologies and self-
explanations. What difference does any of it make? There
are people who make you want to take a broom and
sweep half of their words out the door. I won't say that
Theo Stein is the worst of them, but you certainly can't
call him stark. True there is something forceful about
him, but it is not the kind of forcefulness that I like. I
don't know why people wonder so at my stubbornness.
I'm stubborn about a lot of things. The idea of that
woman at the Sick Fund, looking for solutions for me.

*A*ll this happened years ago, and I'm only mentioning it
now because there is a connection between Theo Stein
and my chairs. Just last week we stood chatting by the
Israel Museum, praising the gardeners for doing such
splendid work for us. The trouble with all this splendor,
though, is the foolishness it has led to. A custom has
sprung up in Jerusalem that whenever a young lady gets

married, she comes to be photographed among the flowers in her fancy bridal clothes, her young man hopping after her. The photographer stands or lies among the flowers and snaps the happy couple from every angle, more her than him: the Hall of the Scroll is a halo for her head, the Valley of the Cross a vanquished backdrop at his feet, then both of them, all flowers, buttons, and bows. They make the whole place ridiculous and depart amid a popping of flashbulbs as if they were movie stars.

Theo Stein and I were in the middle of talking when we saw an unusual sight: a bride dressed all in white, coarse-faced, a cigarette stuck in her mouth, was driving a car very fast by herself with her veil thrown back over her head and an expression of undisguised rage on her face. We had no idea where she was coming from, or where she was going to, or why she looked so annoyed, or why there was no one to drive her to her destination on such a day. If Theo Stein and I were the laughing type, we might have laughed. But we didn't.

"Just so, just so," said Theo Stein, "there are all kinds of conquerors."

The ravens sat on a rock that bore the sign "Kiryat David Ben-Gurion" as though it were a coffeehouse of theirs, and mocked in Latin. Theo Stein stood by my side and sniffed a branch of rosemary that he had picked in the Valley of the Cross. It had a good, dry, sharp smell. Suddenly he asked if he might come to drink coffee at my house some day, because coffee like mine he had drunk nowhere else but my kitchen. The thought of Theo Stein and me in my kitchen disconcerted me, and, in any case, my kitchen had no chairs. Six weeks had passed since I'd

brought them to be fixed and I still hadn't gone to re-
trieve them, so unpleasant were my memories of the
place and of the squat woman who had caused me to lie.
I had no chairs. I was used to not having chairs, the
things that are annoying are the things that one has, not
the things that one doesn't. And without the chairs to sit
on, my kitchen seemed larger and cleaner. What really
did I need them for? I could always grab a slice of bread
and drink a cup of coffee standing up.

I told Theo Stein lamely that my kitchen was empty
at the moment. Once I had my chairs back, I'd be glad
to have him over, why not? He noticed my hesitation
and must have thought that I didn't want him because of
the last time he had come. He exchanged a few more
words and went his way, smelling the rosemary.

*T*his episode prompted me to go the next day for my
chairs. How long, after all, can one put off doing what
has to be done? Moreover, I decided that as soon as I had
the chairs I would call Theo Stein on the telephone at
work to invite him. On the whole I'm not one to use the
office phone for private calls, who is there for me to call
anyway, but a single exception to the rule couldn't hurt.

I returned to the vaulted alley and walked the full
length of it looking for the little workshop. There was no
lack of shops: I passed a jeweler's shop, a shoemaker's
shop, and the shop of a man who sold plastic toys and a
few kitchen utensils, but I couldn't find the shop I was
looking for. The noise was its usual deafening self. Drills
whined, saws rasped, yet my shop was nowhere to be
found. I walked up and down the narrow street several
times without understanding how could I be wrong, be-

cause I knew the street well, from childhood in fact, and couldn't possibly be lost. I shut my eyes halfway and tried walking blindly in the hope that my legs would be better guides, but this didn't help either. The shop was not there.

I opened my eyes again. A young man stood sawing something by a table in the sun. The chips flew all around him, but he was not the same young man I had talked to, nor was the shop across from him the dark, sunken den I remembered. It was a regular store, painted a fresh, bright color inside, with some light-colored, rustic furniture standing in the doorway. I understood now why the shop had eluded me. It was because the vaulting covering the alley had been torn down at this point, so that sunlight was everywhere. When the light changes, places change with it and become unrecognizable. I was standing in light when all the time I had been looking for darkness.

I asked the young man sawing wood what had happened to the repair shop that had been here. He didn't know.

"Have you been working here long?" I asked.

"I just started. Maybe the manager knows."

He wiped his hands on his pants and went inside with me to ask the manager. I hadn't meant, God forbid, to interrupt his work, but he must have wanted to take a break himself, or else was curious. The manager of the store was a young man too, with a plump and nimble appearance and a politeness that seemed to come less from the heart than from the calculation that it paid to be polite. Two or three gold rings adorned his fingers. He had no idea what had happened to the shop's previous owners. He too was new here. He was an agent for Mr.

Urfalli, whom I had no doubt heard of if I was an old Jerusalemite, the same Urfalli family that owned shops and whole streets all over the city. Mr. Urfalli was a hard taskmaster, but well worth sticking to. How did the saying go? If you rubbed up against big money, some of it was sure to rub off on you. As a matter of fact, he remembered now having heard something when moving in here, some business about the police — there had been blows, someone had a stroke, he wasn't really sure. As Madam knows, when you associate a man with trouble, you no longer remember if he was the victim or the culprit. The less said about it, the better. Why rehash ancient history? Yes, perhaps there were some old shabby items left behind when the shop changed hands. No doubt they were thrown out long ago, Mr. Urfalli wouldn't have kept them. Chairs? Old ones? Of straw? But what did I want with straw chairs? I wasn't an old woman, after all, that I needed to be attached to old things. Whoever was young at heart deserved to have something new — and he could tell by looking at me that I was nothing if not young at heart. If I would just step this way to look at his stock, I would forget all about my straw chairs. Perhaps I would like something made of beech? Or of teak? Spanish-style was all the rage now.

Since he was courteous and not ill-natured, I asked him if he knew where I could find the group of old people who had done wicker work for the shop. Perhaps the chairs had been given to them before whatever it was that had happened with the police. He didn't know, but being eager to please he telephoned a friend in another store, which belonged to Mr. Urfalli too, and soon had

the address for me: a workshop by the old-age home in
Kiryat Yovel. A Jerusalemite like myself should have no
problem finding it. The old-age home was in an old
house on a hill where once had been the Arab village of
Bet-Mazmil. There were new housing projects there
now, but the old house still stood. It had the kind of
doors with high thresholds that don't suit old people at
all, an old person had trouble lifting his leg that high, he
might even break it, worse luck, and broken bones were
no joke in old people. On the other hand, it was said that
the thresholds had been put there on purpose to keep the
old people from running away. Everyone knew that old
people sometimes lost their memories and couldn't even
recall their own names. Then the whole police department had to be called out to look for them, which was
a huge waste of public funds. Good luck, Madam, he
said, I've got to hand it to you, and I'm sure we'll see you
again here, even if it's just to visit and see the new stock.

I took the bus to Kiryat Yovel. I found the old-age
home, hidden among tall new buildings whose balconies
on every floor were draped with wash hung out to dry.
It was probably just as well, because if it weren't for the
wash I might have thought I was looking at an army bar-
racks, God forbid. It's good that people have at least their
own private wash. When I reached the old-age home, I
discovered that it wasn't an ordinary day there; a party
was going on in the workshop. A woman with black
hair, which came to a point on her forehead, and a flat,
white face like a barn owl's intercepted me at the door.
Not that I couldn't enter, I certainly could, I could even
drink a glass of cocktail juice, really I was welcome — but

it would be impossible to ask about my chairs until the party was over. When would the party be over? There was no way of knowing: once the old people began to celebrate, it was hard to get them back to their beds. "Far be it from me to begrudge them a little pleasure in life," said the owl woman. "They suffered plenty before coming here, and they haven't much time left. Let them enjoy themselves while they can."

I stepped inside. The back wall was covered with an Israeli flag. Flowerpots filled with sparse, sleepy plants decorated the other walls, rubberplants and philodendrons and Wandering Jew. The old men and women looked well. They stood or sat or hopped gingerly in one place with bright smiles. A few wore colorful cardboard dunce caps strapped to their bald heads, which upset me, because I don't like old people to play the clown. No one ever saw my father or grandfather in an undignified moment, and no one will ever see me in one either. Yet there was nothing base about it, just a kind of childishness, as though they wished to announce with the same beaming countenances that they no longer counted for anything in life, that they had long since renounced all tastes, beliefs, opinions, and disagreements, and were left only with the sunbeams dancing on their cheeks, with party cake and party juice, yum yum. How could I possibly ask what had happened to my vanished straw chairs? One old man came up to me and urged me to eat a piece of cake, my child, my child. I ate a bit to please him and walked out, feeling very out of sorts. I had forgotten about the high thresholds and would have tripped on one of them as I left had the barn-owl woman not gripped me by the elbow. Her hand was very cold. I was frightened.

I didn't know what to do. It was nearly evening and the sun was low in the sky. It occurred to me that I didn't even know what was happening at Authors House that night. Ever since that foolish lie I told I'd been going there less and less, as though the shame of it were written on my face. It seemed to me that the truth was very near and that only my own blindness kept me from seeing it. Perhaps I should try to sleep, I told myself, perhaps I'll dream the answers that can't be found in waking life. My kitchen looked terribly empty without its chairs. There could be no question of inviting Theo Stein—God in heaven, not even to have any chairs! For a moment I thought of returning to the plump, foxy man in the alley, Mr. Urfalli's henchman, and ordering some beechy-teaky from him. Even though it wasn't really me and never could be. Give in, give in, everything seemed to be telling me, don't be such a stubborn old maid, the world likes compromisers. One way or another I saw that the crack in the kitchen wall that I had refinished so carefully was back again. The problem was apparently not just the paint, but a structural fault in the wall itself, which was a much more complicated matter. Bigger solutions are called for, I said out loud to myself, without having the vaguest idea of what they might be. My straw chairs, which I had already given up on, floated before me in space in a slow, weightless dance.

Translated by Hillel Halkin

A Matter of Identity

The two women came at the end of the day. Winding stairs brought them to the lawyer's office, on the top floor of an old Jerusalem building. In the next room was a newspaper cutting agency, and then came the conveniences from which the smell of Lysol spread far and wide. They both puffed their way up till they got there.

"Here it is," said the older woman with a triumphant flourish. She had a flattish, distinctively Slavic face that was somewhere between innocence and a kind of pugnacity. She was one of those women whose body is not important because her actual presence means more than her shape. There she was, puffing and panting, raising her voice, waving her arms, always doing something, plucking a chicken, or cutting material with a sure hand, or dandling a baby. Always doing.

The dim light on the stairs went out. The woman groped for the phosphorescent button, but nobody had bothered to fix one on the upper floor. Or maybe it had peeled off or was out of order. Her hand collected white-wash and tiny bits of plaster. She wiped it once and again on her skirt with the motions of a peasant woman, and said to the younger woman, in Russian:

"Well, how about it, are we to enter in the dark? Go down, darling, go down and give us a little light."

"I wouldn't bother," said the other in a voice that carried constant dissatisfaction and complaint. And at that moment the door of the lawyer's office opened and a client emerged.

The older woman's face lit up. She placed her hand on the lintel of the door to make sure it did not close and leave her in the dark again.

Behind a counter sat a lean, long-toothed woman clerk with her bag open in front of her, making up her face in a compact mirror, getting ready to leave.

"We to the lawyer come," the woman explained in a clumsy Hebrew. She seemed to have grown a little smaller in the presence of the clerk, who shrugged her shoulders — her mouth was pursed in a kind of open triangle, ready for the lipstick — as she pointed toward the inner room. The two entered, and the older woman introduced herself and her daughter.

*I*n the neon light the lawyer examined the daughter's face. She was like the mother, yet unlike her. The pugnacity in her face was less innocent, more aggressive. She was weaker than her mother, not so good. She was wearing a ready-made rose-colored blouse and a snake-green skirt. Over her shoulder hung a chain with a plastic bag at the end. She ought to be wearing plastic sandals with gold or silver straps, but here came a surprise: she was wearing good leather shoes. Must have received them from the lady for whom she works, thought the lawyer, and she doesn't know how to look after them.

He wasn't particularly happy at their arrival. He was tired after a long day, and that evening he had to join his weekly group. It was his practice to meet several friends in a private seminar for expert discussions on Jewish law, and he did not want to be late, even though they had had mighty little to say about law in recent years and had exchanged jokes and scandal instead. They had all grown older.

"I heard that Mister Lawyer Russian speaking," said the woman hesitantly, in Hebrew of a sort.

"I speak it."

"Thank the Lord, my dear," she promptly went on in Russian. "It's hard for me to explain it all in Hebrew. Here's this daughter of mine, she was born to me in Russia. Me, Mister Lawyer, I'm a Russian soul from Krementchug Province, and during the war my fiancé, Stepan, just got lost on us and left me in the family way. Afterward I got to know a Jewish man there, a refugee, Perlmutter they called him, and together we traveled around so much, so much, we got as far as Turkestan, and there my daughter was born to me. And after that my new fiancé, namely Perlmutter, he wanted to go to Palestine, to Israel that is, and we went with him. We didn't have an easy life here, oh no. We lived in a convent, and Perlmutter ran away. Yes, ran away, that's what he did. I always say, why did he bring us with him if he wanted to run away? But that's what he did. You find such people in the world. And so my daughter grew up like that, and now she's a big girl."

"If you want me to look for this Perlmutter—" said the lawyer impatiently.

"No, no, what do I want Perlmutter for? I never got married to him and I haven't anything in common with him. Let him go his way and we'll go ours. That's the way things are. Only there's one thing: my daughter wants to go to Canada. And I said, good, you want to go, to find yourself a new life—go in peace. Only when we went to the consulate, they told us it isn't clear who she is, what her identity is officially, that means, whether she's Perlmutter's or Stepan's or whose. I explained, I explained, and they didn't understand. And they didn't want to give her a visa. They just didn't want. That's why we are here, Mister Lawyer. That's to say, you understand the law, and you'll find us the identity of my daughter so the consul will permit her to go to Canada, and we'll wish you good health."

"That can be checked out in the population register," said the lawyer. "You have the right to go there yourself. Why waste your money?"

The woman flapped her arms in alarm.

"What do I understand of all that Population, Mister! You go, you check for us in that Population, and we'll pay you your fee, and depart in peace."

The lawyer rang for his clerk, but she had already vanished. Her time was up. So he sat down at a neighboring table with a typewriter, and with two fingers tapped out a power of attorney. The glass that covered the little cabinet of law books rang sharply to every letter he struck, and the girl stared at the glass with childish curiosity. She put her finger on the quivering glass and the ringing stopped. The phenomenon interested her. Again and again she tried to block the vibrating glass with her finger, and she felt sorry when the typing was over, staring at her finger for a long time.

Her mother signed in a slow, Cyrillic script, wherever he pointed. She gave her address: an old convent in the north of the city. There she was doing everything, she said, cleaning up and buying greens for the convent; and there she had a little room to this day.

The lawyer fixed an appointment with them, rose, and began to lock up. The woman wanted to go on talking to him on the way, since she rarely had an opportunity to speak Russian outside her convent; but he didn't like talking to clients after finishing their business. He waited a few moments till their footsteps could no longer be heard, then he put out the light and went down himself.

Near the stairway was a grocery shop, a focus of light and life in the murky Jerusalem evening. He entered and bought rolls and the daily cheese ration for his cat. In its kitten days it had caterwauled a great deal, and he had named it Katzenbach, meaning: the Bach of all the cats. But since then it had fattened up and was quiet.

Out in the street, on the way to his car, the lawyer wondered why the woman should be so ready to have her daughter go off to Canada. Most mothers try to keep their daughters at home. And all the more since this mother was all alone.

"The news isn't very good," said the lawyer gravely to the woman, who came alone this time without explaining her daughter's absence. "I inspected the population register. To begin with, your daughter's a minor."

"Well yes, of course," said the woman. During the war she was born, of course she is a minor. Sixteen years old. But she's a clever girl, and a worker too. She'll manage nicely in Canada. Yes."

"And second, she's registered as Perlmutter's daughter."

"My dear, and how would you have me register her? Wartime it was, and where could a woman go all alone with a bastard baby? Perlmutter was living with me then, we ate together, we slept together, we came to Palestine together with him, to Israel that is. And how should I register her if not by his name?"

"Well, nobody's blaming you," said the lawyer. "But because of that registration your daughter can't go to Canada without the permission of her father, or the one who is registered as her father. And that means Perlmutter."

The woman was shocked.

"How is that? How can it be like that, Mister Lawyer? That isn't justice. Did he bring her up? He didn't bring her up, he ran away. But I didn't run away anywhere, I didn't abandon her, poor bastard, I brought her up, and now he has the power to decide whether she is to go to Canada or not? And where can I go searching for Perlmutter now, tell me? These fifteen years I haven't found him. Maybe he's abroad."

"Now look," said the lawyer, "your daughter is registered as the daughter of a Jewish father, that of Perlmutter, whether it's correct or not. Which means she is half-Jewish, and as a minor she can't leave the country unless her Jewish father agrees. That's the law."

"What Jewish father, Lord God in heaven?" wondered the woman. "But she's Stepan's, not Perlmutter's, and Stepan wasn't a Jew, only my boy in Krementchug Province, no, he never was a Jew, *he* wasn't." She leaned toward him and said once again, very clearly, as though talking to a deaf man: "She is from Stepan, not from Perlmutter."

"I believe you," said the lawyer drily, "but that's the law."

"Yes, it's the law," the woman suddenly agreed. "What's to be done, my dear, maybe we should look for Perlmutter. Don't worry, Lawyer darling," she said to the lawyer, "you can go to sleep quietly, I'll find him. I'll find him and I'll get permission from him."

"And if he doesn't give it?"

"Well, God will aid us," said the woman. Though she had accepted the situation, she still looked astonished.

"Only that this law should be like that, well, well! Who would expect such a thing! The law isn't fair, really it isn't fair."

The lawyer looked at her with some annoyance. For some reason he found it hard to picture the girl whom he had seen in his office as being half-Jewish; but it seemed to him that the woman could not know for certain whose daughter she was. Maybe there was something Jewish about her after all, maybe she was the fortuitous daughter and granddaughter of some Perlmutters or other, the granddaughter of woodsmen or innkeepers. Maybe she was of Khazar stock. Who could know? There are so many Perlmutters in the world. Maybe she had received from him those evasive eyes, that floury pallor. Once upon a time people had known their ancestry and the families to which they belonged. A match and marriage had involved several families. Nowadays everything was at sixes and sevens. And here was this girl with her frizzled hair, her makeup, and her plastic, who didn't even know who she was and who her father had been. That wasn't how things ought to be, he thought. A man has to know what his fathers did before he was there.

The lawyer himself had neither wife nor child. He was a tall, thin, willowy man with ivory skin and carefully tended nails, about seventy years old, exceedingly clean, wearing gold-rimmed pince-nez, which surprisingly were just coming back into fashion. Since his branch of the family was coming to an end with him, he was very much concerned with his own pedigree for the sake of his sister's children, who did not in the least care who they were. He considered that it was his function in life to make matters clear to those who were not interested, to help people to see the light and the law, to fight against the chaos that continuously tries to steal back cunningly into people's wills and unchecked desires.

Be all that as it may, Perlmutter had to be found.

The woman brought Perlmutter's address in less than a week. If he had run away, he certainly had not run very far. All this time he had been living in a Tel Aviv suburb, in one of the housing projects built by impatient people with little money to spare, on flat land, where the roofs were flat and had sun-heaters on top of them. She had obtained his address from acquaintances. Only three days she looked and had already found him. So the lawyer sat down and wrote him a letter carefully explaining the whole issue. He enjoyed writing such letters, in which each detail is clarified, as though the order of writing and the exposition inevitably led to the next act.

Nothing happened for a fortnight, and then the postman brought a large commercial envelope containing a letter, written in Hebrew, to be sure, but in Latin characters.

Adoni, said the letter, *ani lo maskim.* Sir, I do not agree.

Perlmutter had plenty to say for himself. He wrote that he suffered a great deal with his liver and had married a widow with a little shop and was not making a living, and he was an unlucky fellow, and all these years he had been longing for his daughter and now she had been found at last, was he likely to let her go abroad? On the contrary, he himself would go to court and demand that she should be his daughter in all respects, just like everybody else's daughters. Let her come to visit him and he would go to the cinema with her. And let her visit them when the holidays came round and eat chicken soup with dumplings like everyone else. And just because of his bad fortune and because he hadn't seen her for fifteen years, did that mean he had no more rights? A father is a father.

The Latin script took the lawyer quite a time to decipher, for he wanted to be sure he understood everything correctly and made the necessary distinction between *lo* when it meant "no" and *lo* when it meant "his," and recognized all kinds of other differences that are perfectly obvious in Hebrew orthography. This manner of writing worked him up. He took a sheet of paper himself and began to write in reverse Hebrew letters, from left to right, and afterward the other way round, in mirror writing. He could still remember the days when he had reversed the direction of his writing from the left-to-right of Russian to the right-to-left of Hebrew. Indeed, he had actually engaged in mirror writing for several weeks. His parents and teacher had worked hard to make him understand the difference; and then, because he had

forcibly compelled himself, he had at last become an expert. Now, after more than sixty years had passed, he
saw that he could still write mirror writing, and rapidly
at that; and the shape of the letters actually seemed more
familiar to him than the standard Hebrew script.

Then he felt alarmed at the hidden strength of things
that are back-to-front. He tore up the sheet as though he
had been poking his nose into matters that did not concern him.

"Good, you go to Perlmutter," the woman agreed,
"only I won't go. You go, Mister Lawyer, and the girl
can go with you, and my husband as well."

"Your husband?"

"Good God, of course my husband! What did you
think, I would stay alone all these years after Perlmutter
ran away?"

"And who's your husband?"

"You'll get to know him in the car. He's a good fellow, a Pole, in Anders's Army he was, and he was
wounded as well; and deserted what's more, poor fellow,
and he hid himself away. And he was starving. He's
suffered a great deal in his life. A gardener he is, he helps
the municipal gardeners many years already. He's
strong—oho, how strong! Other gardeners just scratch
a bit on top and go and plant at once, they haven't any
strength or patience. But nothing like that for him. He
digs, he doesn't leave a root or weed. That's how it is, a
good man is our Piotr, a handsome fellow, not one of
those who goes around promising and promising and
promising and then runs away."

"When did you marry him?"

"Not so long ago, Mister Lawyer. Four or five years maybe."

(So that was the picture: a dark convent and a Pravoslav wedding with a golden crown held over the head of the bridegroom and a golden crown held over the head of the bride, and a ribbon joining their hands together, and nuns bringing an embroidered tablecloth as a gift, with a living chicken, which Piotr would slaughter tomorrow or the day after, and grape jam made in the convent. And the fragrance of wrinkled apples. And incense.)

"In other words, your marriage to Perlmutter was annulled and you've married again?"

"Now Mister Lawyer, look here. I never married Perlmutter, it just came about during the war, we were yearning and longing so much in Turkestan, it was so sad there in Turkestan, people would sooner eat together and sleep together than everyone go separately like a dog. They had houses there, such little ones, like cabins, with walls of earth and thatched roofs. And mud between the houses, and war, war all the time. The front wasn't near us, of course, but someone on his own could starve plenty. Easier by two it was. Sometimes one of us found a little goat milk, sometimes the other worked for a farmer and brought back a few potatoes. We lived. We had a little joy at heart, that's true, but we never spoke about it, only in the evenings. When times are hard it's better by two. I never thought then I'd have such trouble with that Perlmutter, by my life I didn't."

*H*e closed his eyes and could see. Both of them wrapped up in shawls and old faded fringed kerchiefs on account of the cold. Their ears were covered over, there was newspaper inside their boots as they moved bent-backed through the mud in the sad little Turkmeni town, with a rough-edged little tin holder for food, or maybe half a loaf, under the arm.

She was a wind-blown, largish Slav peasant woman, blue-and-milky and yellow as a harvest day, with the scent of milk still in her breasts even when she was shriveled with war, a strong girl and not bad, not at all bad but with a voice like so many Russian women, strong and shrill, and a harsh pronunciation. As for him, he was a refugee Jewish youngster, eyes close together, bent-backed, always wearing a cap, with a funny way of walking, part goat, part human being, not liking to shave, half his strength in his tears. Something within him was permanently closed to her, and that was exactly what attracted her, piercing her soul and forcing her to love him. She was gravid with both of them together, him and the daughter, and never found it hard. Day after day a train would pass near the village without stopping — for why should it stop at such a godforsaken little place? — and in the train were soldiers going home and coaches full of wounded, and the chairman of the local council speaking up for the Party and the Leadership and from time to time passing out something like an official gazette. And the children slanty-eyed, wearing embroidered head-covers like bright playing-balls sliced in half, they talk Russian at school, but they talk Turkmeni with grandmother. And on the First of May, in spite of the war, they manage to lead a sort of procession into the sad brown village square, with flags of deep red with yellow lettering, big flags those are, covering the muddy walls. And tea. Lots of tea.

In snowy weather the woman and her Jew Perlmutter lie under all their pillows and coats, their bodies fitting together like two spoons in a drawer; and even if rivers and plans were weaving together in his head, and even if he was repeating witch-words to himself, like Amu Darya and Amazon and Rio Grande, he would be pressing closer and closer against her, like an abandoned cub nuzzling against its twin.

A goat bleating through the snow. And the odor of feathers. And the smell of cold. And the train. And sleep.

The lawyer sighed.

"All right, we'll fix a date for next week, we'll write and tell Mr. Perlmutter we are coming. And you — don't you want to come? Are you sure?"

"I'm sure, of course I'm sure. What do I have to look for with him? God give him everything good, but he's one thing, I'm another. And my Piotr doesn't want me to go either. You, says he, you stay at home, we'll fix it all up between us men. Only I'll take the daughter, says he, if Mister Lawyer says that's right. We believe in Mister Lawyer like our own father."

What am I to do, thought the lawyer. Am I to fetch this big fellow Piotr to that man with his liver in that Koppel Quarter, or wherever it is he lives, and who knows whether he isn't going to beat him up? And because of me. Between men, that is.

"Listen, your Piotr isn't going to use his hands?"

The woman was shocked:

"God forbid, Mister Lawyer, what are you thinking, my dear? Why, he's a holy angel. Put someone like him on a place that hurts and all the pain will vanish. He has planting hands, green fingers. He wouldn't hit anybody, not even a fly my Piotr wouldn't hit. And yet he's strong—oho! You wouldn't believe it. If you'd see him working out in the open, he lifts half a garden patch with a single blow, even though he isn't young. Women come to watch him when he's working in the municipal gardens, like to a show they come. Such a lovely back he has. So strong."

And that is why she wants her daughter away in Canada, thought the lawyer. Even if she herself doesn't know it. The same urge that led her to take to her heart the thin Jew who had found himself with her in the Turkmeni village was now causing her to decide wisely: one woman in the house and no more. Let the one who isn't married go away.

*B*y chance the lawyer happened to be in the municipality that day and asked questions. An acquaintance told him that from time to time they did actually take on a gardener named Piotr, a queer fellow. Only he had not deserted from Anders's Army, but had been discharged, because he was a hopeless case of mental retardation.

*I*n the evening the daughter stood waiting for the lawyer down below beside the grocery shop. She had clearly been there a long time. As soon as she saw him she came up and began walking at his side, as though accompanying him. She spoke Hebrew.

"Why were you waiting down there instead of coming up?"

"What should I come up for?"

"But suppose I hadn't gone to the office today?"

She shrugged her shoulders.

"I want to go to Canada."

"Why do you think you'll find things better there than here?"

"Look, there's nobody who'd ever marry me here."

He was taken aback.

"Why?"

"Who would marry me?" she snapped bitterly. "A Jew? A Christian? A Russian? An Arab? One of your people? I leave a bitter taste with the boys."

He looked at her and tried to make a picture for himself. Here was this girl with the shrunken breasts, bitter; yet if only someone wanted her, if some joy were to touch her, something in her would be capable of soaring aloft. Then there would be meaning even to the physical bitterness and the horrible clothes from the market stall, and the essential thing would remain: a strong young girl in colorful clothing.

Meanwhile she tripped along the pavement, her expensive neglected shoes dragging because of a worn heel.

"I don't know who I am or what."

"Your mother says—"

"My mother says all kinds of things. She says my father was a Russian soldier."

"Why don't you believe her? I think she's telling the truth. Many things like that happen during a war. Nobody is to blame. He went off to the front. Maybe he was killed. If he hadn't disappeared, you'd be living in a village near Krementchug now, with your mother and your father."

"I'm a double orphan," said she.

"Meaning—Perlmutter?"

"He as well. He was there, and he went away."

"What difference does Perlmutter make to you? He was just a boyfriend of your mother's during the war, when times were hard. Your father was killed in the war against the Germans. You are not the only one."

She didn't even listen to him.

"All right, why didn't she marry him?"

"Stepan? or Perlmutter?"

"What do I care which? Who'll want me now? They are sure to say—that one, she's just like her mother."

He wanted to tell her she was wrong, that in our society . . . and gave up.

"That's why I want to go to Canada. There they don't know all this business, war and all the rest of it. There there are no tricks. There I can even get to know an intelligent fellow. Look at my mother, went and married the town idiot. She didn't have any choice either."

He could understand that desire for an established world so well. He also loved a protected life that moved gently according to plan, with institutions already established, containing something divine, orderly, purposeful. For a moment he thought that maybe he would adopt her as his daughter and give her an identity. But then he saw her ugly face, the iron tooth in her mouth, her childish, menacing insistence on belonging; and he knew that he would never be able to go through with it. She is a case for a sociologist, he said to himself, for a welfare worker, but not for me. Perhaps he would talk about her to his group.

"Maybe I could work in your office?" she said all of a sudden, not believing her own words.

"Doing what? . . . Typing—"

"I can learn," she suggested.

"But how? My clerk has been with me five years—six—"

"Maybe you'll need someone sometime. She may become ill. Anything can happen."

"No, no."

Promptly and without hesitation she descended a whole hope.

"Then maybe you need a housecleaner?"

"My housecleaner has been with me these twenty-five years."

She persisted with the forceful innocence of a sixteen-year-old:

"Maybe she'll die."

"No, no."

Now he sensed that this was a weed in his garden, menacing all that grew there. He stood still.

"Don't worry," he told her. "You can go home. I promise to do everything possible to get you to Canada."

She looked at him with a kind of contempt, as though this dolt did not understand what she was talking about all the time.

"So I should go away?"

"You go along and don't worry, young lady." He closed his world to her with the utmost courtesy, clearly sensing human failure in all this and therefore doubly courteous.

The child was not fooled. She raised her shoulders with a sharp, contemptuous, and despairing motion and went away.

*T*hey took an interurban taxi service. As usual the lawyer had booked himself a place beside the driver. He did not always feel well when traveling and hated to be crowded among others. He himself no longer drove outside town. The speeds required seemed to demand too much of him.

Piotr and the girl sat behind speaking Hebrew, for they both spoke very poor Russian. Yet while a foreign accent could not be noticed with her, the Polish background sounded clearly as he spoke; and they were both short on vocabulary. They would round things off with a gesture or a guess.

A man sitting next to them who looked like an old teacher was polite to them with enthusiastic Zionism: they were new immigrants, doubtless, who had to have the road described to them. Piotr and the girl, who had been perfectly familiar with the road for at least fifteen years, remained politely silent and did not correct him. As for the lawyer, he felt depressed and trapped. It seemed to him as though something in the logical structure of the universe had gone awry ever since those two women had come to his office late that evening. The world had become a thoroughgoing mix-up. No one was like his ancestors. Anything might happen.

When they got out in Tel Aviv, the elderly teacher hoped they would find their own place in Israel and earnestly implored them not to be alarmed at the difficulties. All of us, he said, once found it very hard to be here. We lived in tents, we built roads. And you'll do well if you go to an *ulpan* and learn Hebrew. Things will be all right. What counts is that you are at home. Nobody is going to threaten you here.

Piotr, a sentimental man, found his eyes filling with tears. Quite right, he said to the teacher, quite right, sir, this is a good country, there's nothing to fear from any-body. And as for the Arabs, God will be our aid.

*T*hey took a taxi and made their way to what the lawyer had already grown accustomed to calling the Koppel Quarter in his own mind. It had been built in a hurry and was already pretty much of a slum, with peeling stair-wells, balconies sticking out of the houses like drawers from a plundered cupboard, all kinds of things hanging down from them. The whole quarter was not so much an exterior as the great overturned interior of a flop-house. There was a Bulgarian sign above a cobbler's shop. A dreadful barbershop with a stench of artificial violets. Television antennas. Sand between the houses.

Years before, someone had planted white and pink vincas in front, but nobody had ever bothered to water them and they had shriveled up. Now all that grew in front were chewing gum wrappers, ice-cream sticks, dirty absorbent cotton, and pages of exercise books. In the evenings, there would be watermelon and sour milk containers, thought the lawyer to himself, and the daily journey crowded in the bus all the way to the heart of Tel Aviv and back, to sit in an undershirt and listen to the radio. Summer would be hard in this quarter, harder than the summers of Jerusalemites. A noisy quarter. Any number of radio sets blaring. And people crowded far too close, the warmth of one reaching the warmth of the next, voice touching voice, one man's smell in the other's nose. The walls were an illusion, or maybe a grudging concession to the concept of civilization.

If the lawyer expected the girl to show any special feeling at Perlmutter's house, he was wrong. Her face did not change but grew even harder, with its somewhat malicious obstinacy and unresolved dissatisfaction. She was outside it all and above it all. Her hair shone with a sticky spray from the hairdresser's and looked like a sort of mouse nest rolled up on the back of her head. She wore a dress of flimsy material, the kind that is sold at bargain prices on market stalls at the end of the season. Had there been the slightest trace of ease and freedom in her appearance, it could even have suited her. But that eternal sulkiness of hers, that shackled and closed quality of stupid women, caused the light dress to seem like a piece of armor. She did not seem to move her arms at all, as though they were tied to the body, and only her shoulders jumped up and down in a wild and nervous motion depending on her mood. She looked like a woman who had never enjoyed a really good day all her life long. The lawyer had to remind himself that she was sixteen years old. To Piotr she spoke in her constantly plaintive voice, but without any tension.

As for Piotr, he was just as he had been described: big, clumsy, careful, with a big Adam's apple, dragging his bad leg and wearing a striped shirt buttoned up to the top without a tie, a jacket over it. He did not wear the collar over the jacket, a gentile habit. He walked beside her as though he were calming her and being conciliatory.

They mounted the steps. Perlmutter opened the door. He was smaller than the lawyer expected, little and creased, with his skin yellow as though it had been damaged by some chemical. There was something slightly rotten in his breath. He seemed to be older than the woman who had been with him in Turkestan, older by no few years. The image of the young, sharp, hungry Jewish boy with the cap no longer suited him, and was replaced by a picture of a Jew who must already have been about forty at the time, with sparse hair and quite a different, more materialistic, bitterness. Maybe he had had a few coins and bits of gold, and some dollars sewn into the lining of his coat, and that was why she had come to him, he thought. What do I know? Perlmutter gave the impression of a petty rogue. He lacked that aesthetic, on-show intensity that you sometimes find in big-league rogues and swindlers who are pleased with what they do.

*P*erlmutter opened his arms to embrace his daughter. She allowed him to hug her for a moment, but when he wanted to kiss her, she pushed him away, her fists clenched.

"Are we coming in or not?" she asked in a vinegary voice. She had definitely made up her mind not to be excited.

"Welcome, welcome, blessings for keeping us alive and sustaining us and bringing us to this day," sobbed Perlmutter. "Rosa! Rosa! My daughter has come! What a day, what a grand day! Fifteen years, Lord Almighty."

Even his tears appeared yellowish.

Rosa, Perlmutter's wife, looked at them all with piercing button-eyes and without a sound offered refreshments: broken squares of chocolate from a large slab, presented in a glass dish. The lawyer looked around. There were two rooms, a balcony, and a tiny kitchen. In the corner stood a big old radio with a glass cat upon it. Four or five bits of electrical apparatus were joined to a single socket, their wires dangling. A Sick Fund bottle stood on the table. An ashtray shaped like a swan, another like a pink hand. And Perlmutter wiping away his tears.

"Look, just look," he urged them, dashing around and fetching heaps of old photos. "This is my former wife at Ula village in Turkestan. And this is me, and here we are together at the First of May celebration. This is the statue of Stalin here. And this is our daughter, the baby. Just look how I kept the photo next to my heart for fifteen years. I remember just like today how she was born. We fetched her mother to the hospital in a cart, and on the way, just imagine, an axle broke, and two soldiers came to help us get there in time, and she was already beginning to give birth on the way, so sure as I am alive. In a hurry she was."

"One moment," said the lawyer. "You said your former wife. Were you married?"

"What do you mean were we married? Of course we were married, what else? I don't say we went to the rabbi, not that, but we had a civil wedding, in Soviet Russia, before the official registrar of marriage — we were registered in the books of the council all fit and proper. And afterward we went to the Cultural Center with some friends, and we had something to drink, and we ate herring. There wasn't much to eat in those days, but we found some good herring. Who says we weren't married? Of course we got married."

"Then Madam Rosa is—"

"She is my wife at the Rabbinate. After we came here and this woman ran away from me to the convent and they wouldn't even let me see her and the child, I asked myself what I should do. It's impossible without a wife. I asked a lawyer, and he told me that such civil marriages don't count and I could marry a wife at the Rabbinate. I went to a matchmaker, I told him I'm ill and can't work much, but as a man — that's okay. So he found me Rosa, who has a shop. We went through with it and here I am."

Rosa, whose natural hair looked like an ancient wig, had brewed strong tea, which she presented in glasses with plastic holders. She never said a word.

"Girlie," Perlmutter turned to the daughter, "tell your father how you are. What are you doing? What are you learning in school? Do you have a boyfriend?"

She drily described her studies at the Mission School, her work as a waitress in the German Colony, and how she wanted to go to Canada.

"What Canada, Lord God Almighty? Canada all of a sudden? God preserve you, girlie, why are you dashing off alone to a foreign country? Why, this is your country, I'm your father."

"Oh, you aren't my father," said the daughter impatiently. "This is all a show. You have to put on a show, the lawyer said, so it's put on."

Perlmutter burst into tears, real tears, with sobbing and shaking shoulders.

"Well, well, you are exaggerating," said Piotr to the girl as he produced a handkerchief to wipe his hands. He had never been so embarrassed in all his life. "You don't have to cry, Mr. Perlmutter, God is merciful."

"I must ask you to behave better," said the lawyer.

The girl shrugged her shoulders.

"Okay, so I'm prepared to behave, but he shouldn't say he's my father."

"How do you know?" the lawyer asked severely.

"Just look, I'm not even like him."

They all looked at the two of them. Indeed, it was hard to find any resemblance, even with an effort. But then she was Stepan's, the lawyer remembered, not Perlmutter's. Perlmutter had only given her his name when she was about to be born in Turkestan. And meanwhile Perlmutter finished weeping.

"That's the way it is, that witch hid her from me for fifteen years, she poisoned her soul, so what do you want her to say now? But that won't help you, do you hear, I'm your father before God and man, you were born to me in summer during the month of August at Ula village in Turkestan, in the hospital, and what's more the axle of the cart broke on the way, so what does your mother have to say to that? Eh?"

*T*he lawyer tried to intervene. He was accustomed to patching things up between people quarreling in his office. Now he began to deliver his solemn and wordy address, appealing to their decency, their human self-respect, their belief in the goodness within them. Even if they did not understand, they would listen for a few moments, as though feeling that in spite of everything there is some higher order in the universe; and they would calm down. This time he delivered his speech in the Koppel Quarter, even though his words were interrupted every moment by a carpet-beater overhead or a mother shrieking at a naughty boy down below. This kind of thing was easier in the office. The lawyer drank his tea and longed for Jerusalem.

After his speech they stopped being rude to one another, although they did not come to terms. Perlmutter

sat over the heap of photos like a miser over coins. It was
hard to understand how he could have taken so many
photos in that village during the middle of the war. Had
it really been possible to obtain film freely? Or maybe
this was one of the questionable businesses he had gone
in for there; so it would seem. Photo was flung on photo,
and in them all was the smiling young woman, or he, or
both of them together, or the baby, or the woman with
her daughter, or he with the daughter, or all three of
them together. There was even a photo of the daughter
lying on her belly, naked on a tiger skin, all fit and
proper. A family album in every respect.

"Then come to visit your father," said Perlmutter.
"Spend a week or a fortnight. I'll take you to the pictures
in Tel Aviv. You'll eat with us on Sabbath. You'll see
how well Rosa cooks. You'll see. Your mother won't
recognize you. You'll get cheeks like an apple."

"I'm going to Canada," the girl burst out as though
she were throwing a stone at him and began to go down
the steps. The lawyer and Piotr came down behind her.

Perlmutter shouted:

"No Canada! No Canada! Not as long as I'm alive!"

*W*hen they came down they found it hard to get a taxi.
What driver would be crazy enough to go to the Koppel
Quarter? Their shoes filled with sand. The girl cried, and
Piotr patted her on the back as though she had swal-
lowed a fish bone: that's enough now, that's enough.

Gulping and choking, she finally climbed together
with them into a bus that pulled up into the sand and hid
her face in a handkerchief. The men were silent. They
could clearly feel that this was a very young girl indeed,

after all. At the central station the lawyer got out and bought her a box of sweets. She opened it at once, eagerly, and began to suck.

"I'm going to kill Perlmutter," she said after the tears.

"*It's* not true," said the woman. "As heaven is my witness and as I hope for salvation, I never married him at all, neither a civil marriage nor any other. I simply lived with him." And then she added something unexpected: "He was a gay fellow, this Perlmutter. I never knew anyone as gay as he was. Only he never liked to work, never."

The lawyer stared at her, at a loss what to do.

"How do you explain his story that you were married?"

She held out her hands on either side.

"I don't know, as heaven's my witness I don't know. But he knows it isn't true, so why should he lie just so? Just to harm people?"

"Maybe you'll meet him and find why he's making all these claims?"

"Piotr won't let me."

He did not know whom to believe. There was a measure of truth in both of them. He knew he would not succeed in finding the real truth. All of a sudden he had an idea:

"Listen. Maybe there's a way out of all this mess. The girl's a minor and there is a problem about her paternity. You are married to Piotr now, a Church marriage I understand. Suppose Piotr adopts the girl?"

"Adopts?" She did not grasp it.

"He can adopt her legally as his daughter, and then

as her adoptive father he can give her permission to go to Canada."

A pair of starry tears appeared in the woman's eyes. She rose and embraced the lawyer's head, and then, as befits a peasant woman, she wanted to clasp him round the knees; but he would not permit it.

"May God give you everything good, sir, I always knew that your cleverness would save us all, may Jesus give you length of days, may the Holy Mother give you good fortune and everything good."

But at the door she turned round, worried:

"And Perlmutter won't object?"

"I don't think he can object. His paternity has not been sufficiently proved, and besides he has abandoned you and the girl for the last fifteen years. The judge isn't such a bad fellow."

*H*er abundant joy affected him as well. He was as chirpy as a sparrow when he went home. That evening he found himself full of energy, removed Katzenbach from his knees and drew up the application for adoption.

*T*he judge said he wanted to see Perlmutter all the same.

*W*hen Perlmutter entered the judge's chambers, the lawyer did not recognize him at first. The wispy sideburns on his cheeks had grown and seemed longer. He was dressed in a white, new shirt, and there was something fresh and reddish, almost blossomlike, in his yellowish color. His whole appearance had changed. He now seemed like a cheerful Hassid. The three of them sat down together: the judge in his armchair in front of the high-piled desk, the lawyer and Perlmutter facing him. The judge and the lawyer had many papers. Perlmutter did not have a single sheet of paper in his hands. Easy and smiling he sat, looking first at one and then at the other.

"Well then, Mr. Perlmutter," said the judge. "You claim that the girl is your daughter?"

Perlmutter produced a sheet of paper from his pocket.

"Your Honor, I found the birth certificate of the hospital in Turkestan. You can see by this document that the mother was registered with my family name and the daughter was registered in my name as my daughter. We were married at the village council office in front of the registrar of marriages, in a civil ceremony. And the daughter is mine, there's no doubt of it."

"How did you manage to get the woman into the hospital in the middle of the war?" asked the lawyer as though cross-examining a witness. "I thought all the hospitals were full of soldiers."

"I had my connections," said Perlmutter obstinately. "And apart from that, Mister Lawyer, you may be an important man, I couldn't say, but even if you are the most important man there is, you can't argue with my documents. Here you are, take a look, all the documents are here."

"The registration is not a proof of paternity in itself," said the lawyer to the judge.

"I understand," answered the judge and turned to Perlmutter. "Look what complications you've caused us, Mr. Perlmutter. You know that according to Jewish law the child follows the mother, and you went and married yourself a non-Jewess, and you've complicated the whole issue as a result."

"A non-Jewess?" Perlmutter started with a loud, victorious voice. "What non-Jewess? Your honor, why, she's a non-Jewess just as I'm a non-Jew. She's a Jewish girl, a full daughter of Israel. And what if she does have blue eyes, so what? Is it written anywhere that a Jewish girl mustn't have blue eyes? Against the law is it?"

*T*he lawyer felt as though the familiar judge's chambers had somehow left the bounds of reality. A concentrated white autumnal light making its way through a gap in the clouds was the only thing that was tangible; and it seemed to him that the scanty light was covering everything, those seated there, the furniture, the piles of paper. Sheets of light drowning everything within, while the people slowly faded away, weakening like a candle flame with the coming of dawn, their strength growing steadily less, a little more and nobody would be aware of them, just a little more and people could pass through them the way a man passes through smoke.

Bemused as he was, he thought: whatever Perlmutter points to and says is Jewish—it's as though he said, "It's mine." As though he had expropriated it. The divine hand of Perlmutter. What can I do against that?

*T*he judge stood up and shifted the heavy curtain to darken the room. The lawyer calmed down a bit. People and objects returned to their normal shapes.

"You realize the significance," said the judge to the lawyer in a low voice. "If the woman really is Jewish as this gentleman claims, then the girl's Jewish as well and I have no authority to issue an adoption order to the mother's husband who is a non-Jew."

"I understand, Your Honor, but I am not convinced of the truth of his statements. It all has to be clarified, it's necessary —"

Perlmutter gazed first at one and then at the other, enjoying himself tremendously. Here was a bomb he had exploded in the judge's chambers! Ever since he left Soviet Russia and the gentiles who could always be twisted round his little finger, ever since his dealings had begun with the Jewish Agency, and the Income Tax, and the Electricity Corporation, he had never succeeded in fixing a man or an institution like this. He seemed to become twenty years younger.

"How do you know she's Jewish?" the lawyer asked.

"What do you mean how do I know? She said so herself. Have you ever seen anybody lying and saying he's a Jew? A Jew may lie and say he's a gentile, that we've seen, but the other way round? Who'd be crazy enough to lie like that in the middle of the war?"

"What do you suggest, sir?" the judge leaned over to the lawyer again.

"We'll clear it up," said he. "We'll hunt for documents one way or the other. This is an absolute surprise for us." He almost added: an act of God.

"Try and ascertain the facts," said the judge, and they left the chambers.

In the corridor the lawyer said; "Listen, Perlmutter, if the woman is really a Jewess, then it's very doubtful whether your present marriage to Madam Rosa can be valid. Why should we complicate matters? Because then they'll charge you with bigamy. That may cost you plenty."

"Well, and what do I care if my marriage to Rosa isn't valid. So it isn't."

The lawyer suddenly realized that Perlmutter had met the woman in secret, in spite of Piotr's prohibition. He looked at him questioningly, but Perlmutter's rascally face gave nothing away except a cunning, opaque, secretive triumph.

*T*hen let us assume he has seen her, and let us assume that something of the old attraction is still left, and let us assume that the earth opened up its mouth and there appeared a new gateway of possibilities, a style of life, a transformation they had not thought of in advance, neither he nor she. And why not, after all? Fifteen years apart, yet he is perfectly familiar with that large white body, and she knows all his habits. Their embrace on the very occasion of meeting caused the bodies to continue on their own before either of them could decide whether or no. And Piotr and the girl suddenly lost their importance. And now he wasn't going to give her up. There's a new situation for you. A few moments of all but forgotten pleasure, and the girl wouldn't go to Canada.

*P*erlmutter leaned over for the lawyer's ear and whispered in Yiddish:

"That Rosa, she's an old maid."

And pranced jauntily toward the buses.

*T*he lawyer was one of those people possessed by an old dream that only a woman resembling him could find favor in his eyes. Since he was tall, ivorylike, and black-eyed, he went looking for someone tall, ivorylike, and black-eyed who would seem to be his, one of his family. In his youth he had searched for his female twin, for his female counterpart, and when he did not find her, he gave up the search. The other, the non-family, fruitful strangeness, did not accord with his capacity. He was not inquisitive, so he remained alone. And hence it was hard for him to understand this whole incident of Perlmutter and the woman. Well then, was she a Jewess or not? Had she met him or not?

*H*e went to the convent. It was a large building with a wall round it in the north of the city. A side entrance between a stone wall and a thick hedge led to a little stone building, a kind of gate-house, where the woman's room was. In the courtyard grew a geranium and hollyhocks. A Jerusalem jasmine, strong and sharp in the rocky dryness, spread its scent afar. Bells were pealing in the convent, whether for prayers or a meal he did not know. The woman and Piotr were both at home. He was eating while she sat beside him, her eyes red with tears. There was no doubt of it. She had been up to mischief with Perlmutter, and Piotr did not know.

She wiped a chair and seated the guest.

"Do you want your daughter to go to Canada?" he asked her sternly.

"I do," said she.

"Then why do you . . . like this . . . "

She wiped her eyes again and again. It was hard to

understand how even Piotr could not realize that this was a sinful, suffering woman. Her hand beat her breast every few moments in a brief automatic movement. Her eyes were red, her hair disheveled.

"Perlmutter won't give up now," said the lawyer without going into details, so that Piotr should suppose he was referring to the daughter.

But Piotr sat, large and smiling, drinking tea in his big khaki working trousers and his striped shirt that was buttoned right up to the neck. Before him lay a chunk of bread, a cucumber, and a radish, all of which he cut up carefully into tiny, equal-sized pieces. All that was going on in the room was as far from him as noonday noises in the airfield of some other country.

"I know, I know, that's my punishment."

"Well, we'll see what can be done," said the lawyer in annoyance. His eyes fell on the narrow iron bed in the corner under the ikon. It was covered with many pillows in the old style. One red pillow had no cover on it. There was an obscenity about it, as though it ought to be hidden. Here Perlmutter had been, he thought, with his ailing liver and his rotten breath. Here all this flesh had moved under a terrifying, genuine, heady urge, concerned with nothing but itself. A man could live his whole life long without knowing that forceful drive even once. There was no appeal. *Vénus à sa proie attachée.* Perlmutter.

"Do something for us, my dear," murmured the woman, after her fashion. "And the Holy Mother will appeal in your favor, the Holy Virgin will entreat for you."

This time she chose only the mother of Jesus as intercessor, as though she could not count on the saints, who are men, to understand her properly.

Piotr rose to accompany him to the gateway. He wiped his hands clean of the cucumber with slow, comprehensive motions, which were absolutely identical with those of the woman. Then he produced a pruning knife from his capacious pocket and cut the lawyer a fine branch of jasmine.

"The scent is good and healthy," he said with a smile. "Jasmine makes you forget trouble."

His words seemed to indicate some glimmer of knowledge, as though something had made its way through the dense cover of his intelligence — but no more than a glimmer. As he stood between the iron gates of the convent, his head humbly bent and his eyes cast down, Piotr was a handsome man.

*T*he lawyer found it hard to fall asleep. It was toward morning when he did so, and he dreamt that a heavy bomber of World War vintage was about to fly, but the runway was a street full of people. When he asked somebody how this could be permitted, the fellow answered that everybody already knew how to be careful with that plane, and no special runway was necessary. He woke up startled and alarmed, feeling as though he had been almost run over.

*T*he lawyer's contacts with the world were usually well balanced. Sometimes he would witness an outburst on the part of clients, or wishes and desires of witnesses; but these could always be checked, either with the aid of that calculated and eloquent speech, or by threats of the law, or by the full authority of court and state. It was rare for him in all his legal experience to face such crazy, humiliating vitality. He felt as though any step he took in this case promptly became something else, as though people had burst into his home and turned it into a fair or a circus. Perlmutter was not the only gay dog, he thought in annoyance, they were all gay, the whole jovial gang — except the girl, the only unfortunate individual in the whole affair, more unfortunate than any person with a sense of responsibility could bear. He very much wanted to transfer the whole case to his assistant, a much younger man who might be amused by the whole business and less concerned as to what was true or not. But it was too late. He knew he would have to finish what he had begun.

Henceforward, however, he decided, he would deal with papers and not with people. His mistake was that he had been involved too much with the people concerned. Now he ordered his secretary not to make any more appointments with any of that gang for the present. Let her tell them that he was busy.

And meanwhile he sat down and drew up an application to the Ecclesiastical Institutions in Moscow, requesting them to ascertain for him whether this woman was a Jewess or not. Never in his life had he had so strong a feeling of doing right as when he drafted formal sentences, sealed the envelope containing the photographs of documents with red wax, selected himself another large thick envelope on which he personally wrote the address with old-fashioned Cyrillic curlicues, and sent the clerk to the post office to register the whole thing. He placed the registration slip in his pocketbook to begin with, then changed his mind and put it in the safe. Now nothing would go wrong, he decided, nothing would go

off the track or surprise him or bring him face to face
with unforeseen facts again.

*T*hat envelope of his would reach Moscow, he thought,
it would be lowered in the postal sack at Vnukovo
Airfield, where by now it must certainly be very cold indeed and postal clerks and porters would be wearing fur
hats; and afterwards the envelope would reach a minor
priest, some secretary doubtless sitting in a cold office of
an old church amid the scent of incense and the flickering
of ikons—no, no, there was no reason for the business
office to have the dim gold gleam of ikons, I am exaggerating, he thought, what must certainly be there is a picture of the heads of state; and after that the young priest
in the black hat with his earlocks and curls sprouting out
all round would present the material to a patriarch, an old
man dressed more ornately and with a curling beard—he
has it curled once a week at the neighboring barbershop—and a big cross on his broad chest and a reddish
bulbous nose and any number of gold rings on his
fingers. The Pravoslav Church loves gold even more
than the Catholic. Doubtless this was a memory of its
Byzantine origin, all the gloom and gold and hidden
treasures and manuscripts and endless intrigue—and
amid all this and above all this, a ceremonial that is the
most splendid in the world, tasting of the kingdom on
earth. The patriarch would take a pen in his hand—who
knows, maybe he has a ballpoint pen by now—and
would write to various regions and districts. Yet why
should he write after all? The Church offices must certainly have telephones too; after all, Saint Mikola and
Saint Onuphrius and all the other faded, gilded thick-

beards had not prohibited the telephone. And then local priests would go searching in church registers and would find a baptismal certificate; and the elders among them would remember. And in the evening the village priest would tell an old man or woman surviving from those times that a letter had come all of a sudden from Israel, from the Holy Land, asking for documents about the daughter of Zakhar and Yevdokia, may they rest in peace. And children would want the stamps from Israel, but the priest would not give them away, being a collector himself.

*A*ll that, thought the lawyer, provided that Perlmutter was lying.

*T*he Russian Church functioned swiftly. Before very long the postman brought a huge packet by registered mail, with ugly Russian stamps, showing satellites in space and the face of Tereshkova, and handsome red seals.

There was a client with the lawyer at the time. He excused himself, went into the next room, and eagerly opened the packet.

The Moscow Church wished peace upon earth to the lawyer and, God aiding, informed him with accompanying documents that the said woman was a Christian daughter of Christians for three generations back at least, her mothers and fathers had been pure and perfect gentiles even in the days of the deceased tsar, and whoever declared otherwise was uttering falsehood, and may God bless all men of truth and peace, amen.

*T*his time Perlmutter brought Rosa to court as well but told her to take a seat in the corridor and wait for him. She sat submissive and opaque, her button eyes not missing a single detail. In front of her passed people quarreling about contracts and wrangling about property, arguing and divorcing one another and complaining, most of them noisy, some of them confused. Rosa sat with her legs apart and waited for Perlmutter.

*T*he judge said severely:

"Mr. Perlmutter, why did you tell us that she was a Jewess?"

Defeated, Perlmutter hung his head:

"That's what she told me, Your Honor, and what should I do? I believed her. You can't check the papers of everybody who tells you something."

The lawyer swiftly set out to clinch his victory.

"Well then, Your Honor, the woman is a non-Jewess and the stepfather is a non-Jew. There can be nothing to prevent the issue of a legal order of adoption in order that the personal status of the girl be finally settled."

"I agree to the adoption," said the judge at length. "Mr. Perlmutter, if you have nothing more to add, you may go."

"I am a sick man," said Perlmutter. "All this excitement—"

"It's better for you this way, Mr. Perlmutter." The lawyer could not refrain from taking revenge. "Your wife is waiting for you outside. She'll look after you, take you home."

"I'm not to blame here," said Perlmutter. His face was yellow. "Believe me, I'm not to blame. I always believe what people tell me. Otherwise it's impossible to live in the world."

He went out dragging his legs. Even before he closed the door, his impatient call in Yiddish to the wife who supported him could be heard:

"Rosa! Rosa! Come here."

Go on, go on, get back to your Koppel Quarter, my friend, thought the lawyer, back to the sour milk and undershirts, back to the old maid, that old button-eyed, buttoned-up saintly reprobate of yours with the legs apart whom nobody has ever seen without earrings and a round brooch. Get along with you and get out of our lives.

*F*rom this point everything was plain sailing. The woman, the girl, and Piotr were summoned to chambers. The order of adoption was issued, signed, and sealed. Piotr, large, mulish, and radiant, pressed the lawyer's hand for a long time and wanted to shake hands with the judge as well. But the latter was the sort of man who does not enjoy physical contact. Piotr did not even notice it and pressed the corner of the writing table instead. The daughter clung to her mother, and both of them blessed the lawyer in several languages and linguistic fragments, until he edged them out of the chambers with nudges and noises, the way a driver of oxen gets a herd of cattle out of the way. There was no sign of Perlmutter or Rosa. They must have gone back home, thought the lawyer, and better that way, far better—you mustn't allow different kinds to get mixed up together, one religion with another or one type of person with other types. All that leads to confusion, to chaos, and that's one of the things that destroys the world.

In the office he called his assistant and told him the whole story; and then, well pleased with himself, he invited the young fellow to a home-fare restaurant on the second floor. Things were back to normal.

In the afternoon fists began banging on the door of the lawyer's office. It burst open even before the clerk got there. In came a huge bouquet of red roses, uniform and coarse, fresh from a flower shop, with the requisite asparagus and the cellophane and the tinsel ribbons. Behind the bouquet appeared a gigantic box of chocolates, the kind the clerk had only seen in plate-glass windows, and which she was sure could only be props. These and other bundles were borne by four people: Piotr, the woman, the daughter, and Perlmutter. They all smelt strongly of liquor, a scent of festival that seemed slightly askew. In her hand the daughter held a large ugly crystal goblet, heavily gilded at the sides and on top and containing a heavy gold spoon of Pravoslav craft. Perlmutter had one bottle of cognac in his hand and another, almost empty, sticking jauntily out of his pocket. It was impossible even to imagine where they had left Rosa. Tipsy as they were, it would have been pointless to ask.

They burst into the room of the lawyer, who was just removing some securities from the safe. Startled, he closed it and found them round and about him. They sat him down, thrust everything into his bosom, and began singing:

"May you live a hundred years, a hundred years!"

"Here, darling, here, brother mine, drink up,"

begged the woman, planting the cognac in front of him.

"In crystal and gold!" piped up the girl to Piotr. "Daddy, fetch it!"

They placed the ugly goblet in front of him and poured him out his measure, so that he couldn't help but drink it. Each of them in turn took a swig at the bottle, which didn't seem to be the first either.

"But ladies and gentlemen, this is a public place, ladies and gentlemen, I thank you, but I can't work like this—"

"May he live a hundred years!"

"Cheers for our lawyer!"

"Long live the State of Israel! A glass for the Church!"

"You all think I don't know the prayers of the Jews?" The woman's face was bright and shining. "And how I know! Shema Isroil, Adoynoy Eloyheinu!" In the Yiddish pronunciation.

"Amen. Amen!"

*T*he clerk stood in the doorway. Piotr offered her his arm in knightly and gentlemanly fashion, to lead her to the table.

"Come, sister," he boomed in Russian. "Come and drink with us, we are rejoicing today."

The bouquet of roses fell. Perlmutter tried to pick it up and lost his balance. He sat on the carpet next to the roses, rolling with laughter. The girl held out her hand to him:

"Stand up, Daddy, that's not nice."

So both of them were daddy. With a sinking heart the lawyer suddenly noticed the girl's thumb, short and hammerlike, was absolutely identical with the thumb of Perlmutter. The same thumb. Truth had fled away, never to return. His eyes grew dark.

"Our lawyer is a sweetie!" yelled Perlmutter in Hebrew from the carpet.

The woman made the sign of the cross over him.

"May your Messiah come soon, and then all the world will be brothers."

"O General, lead us to the sea," sang Piotr in his thick voice in Polish. His voice was too heavy to bear, he dropped a tone and added some false notes from time to time. "Lead us to the ocean v-a-a-s-t!"

"Our lawyer is a sweetie!" yelled Perlmutter again, and this time stood up waving his hands.

"The State of Israel is a sweetie!" said the daughter. She took off her tight shoes and held them in her hand.

"After you, General, we follow and go to the sea so blu-u-u-e!"

"Drink up, my dear, drink up," said the woman wiping away her tears. "You're among brothers and sisters, don't be afraid."

Under duress the lawyer drank again. His head was really whirling by now.

"Shall I call the police?" asked the clerk, grinning broadly and displaying pink gums.

"No, no need, these ladies and gentlemen will calm down by themselves—they'll calm down themselves—just a little water—"

A plaster cast of Dr. Weizmann standing on the lawyer's table fell and shattered.

"May God forgive you, brothers," shrieked the woman. "You came to thank Mister Lawyer and you cause him damage? A lovely white Lenin he had, and they smashed it, they smashed it, the sinners!"

"We'll buy him a statue," said Piotr. "We'll buy him ten statues."

"Our lawyer's a sweetie!"

"To Canada, to Canada! Long live Canada!"

*T*he lawyer was in a state of intoxicated clarity. He felt that he was being carried away as in those distant days when, a vengeful raging kicking child, he had been swept helplessly aloft in the arms of a tall and laughing mother. He had lost his sense of balance. Strangely enough that was both a shame and yet calming. The thin, hard voices of the women, like the voices of angels, the smell of cognac, the clinking of glasses, the flashing of the transparent cellophane, and that otherwhere scent of the roses, all mingled together into a kind of warm sweet blind shameful rising wave that could not be withstood. He admitted—he could see—that something or somebody knew better than he did; but he did not know who, or what there was to know. He was surrounded by smiles, affection, kindheartedness, as though a great big world of handsome and omnipotent adults was once again accepting a naughty boy, and everything had been forgiven him most lovingly, yet what his transgression had been—*that* he could not remember no matter how he tried. He submitted to growing small. The sweet choking shame made him give way completely, drinking, raising his shortsighted, well-meaning eyes to them and responding to their smiles. He knew they had forgiven him but did not know what he had done. He admitted everything. The world beyond his own world was more spacious and sweeter than he had known. Anything could be expected there, including himself and his many reckonings. Nothing was as it should be, and everything was excused. They gave him some more. He drank with pious, concentrated intensity. His eyes clouded with tears of thanksgiving.

At length he rose with shaky knees.

"Good people, I thank you from my heart, I thank you, but go along now, go along, it's getting late—"

All four of them kissed him, two kisses from each, right cheek, left cheek, leaving a strong scent of cognac and rejoicing. It seemed that they could not leave him. Again and again they came back from the door, to thank him afresh, to shake his hands. Perlmutter kissed him all over again.

"We're interfering, enough already, enough, let's go!" said Archangel Piotr.

They departed, their jubilations rising up from the stairwell. The news-cuttings agent from the neighboring room peered in through the doorway and said, cantankerously:

"Mazal tov, I didn't know it was your birthday."

The clerk burst into a fit of laughter.

In the room remained fragments of the bust, the bouquet on the carpet, and the crystal goblet with the spoon. The lawyer felt certain he had never seen such an ugly object in his life.

"Do you want this glass?" he asked the clerk. "If so, take it along."

"But it's expensive," she said with covetous eyes.

He waved his hands:

"Go on, take it. I don't want it. And get the roses out of here as well. This isn't an actress's dressing room."

At length they cleaned up, closed and locked everything. The lawyer had a headache. He even forgot to buy cheese for Katzenbach. The engine would not ignite properly. With a thunderous headache and a sense of universal pardon and forgiveness he arrived home, opened the gigantic box of chocolates, and found that they had gone moldy with age: all were white and turned to powder at a touch. And who would buy such a box, it must have stood in the shop window for twenty years. He collected the lot and flung it into the dustbin. As he bent forward, his insides seemed to heave with all the unaccustomed drinking. Excitement of this kind wasn't for him, he told himself as he rolled up in bed without a shower or supper. Tomorrow was a new day, tomorrow would be different.

*H*e was almost asleep when his belly suddenly began shaking with laughter. He rubbed the sleepiness out of his eyes, sat up in bed, and found himself laughing aloud. It was only part intoxication. The laughter increased and spread like rain after a long drought, more and more. The startled Katzenbach leapt from the foot of the bed and fled into the kitchen.

"But it would be interesting to know," he said loudly to the darkness, "how they managed to get rid of Rosa."

And laughing, laughing endless torrents of laughter, he suddenly yawned spaciously, a liberating yawn, and fell asleep like a stone.

Translated by J. M. Lask

Two Hours on the Road

Past Latrun, between the low hills and the mountains, Ada, without warning, finds herself driving into fear.

Ada slows down. Her foot feels heavy on the gas pedal. She can't drive anymore. Together with her, we feel how stuffy the car is, how the world is boxing her in. Ada quickly turns the handle to lower the window, then raises it again. Ada is very frightened. The cars speeding toward her seem about to veer out of their lane, ballooning in size as they threaten to collide with her.

The car behind her honks a sharp warning and passes her a little too quickly. Ada brakes and pulls off onto the shoulder. She is covered with sweat. The hitchhiking soldier in the passenger seat looks at her in surprise.

"What's the matter?"

Ada shakes her head vaguely to say: nothing.

"Something wrong with the car?" Impatiently. He's in a hurry.

"The car is fine."

The soldier mumbles something that sounds like a curse and quickly bails out to look for another ride, slamming the door behind him. He is sweaty and hatless. The shirt of his fatigues hanging out of his pants does not conceal his paunch. He has no time. Already he is standing by the side of the road with his hand out. Now he is squeezing into the cabin of a pick-up truck that has screeched to a stop, beside two other men. We will get along without him.

The sweat trickles into Ada's eyes and streams from the back of her ears down her collar in a steady flow. Ada feels very bad. Her fear translates into bodily signs. The tips of her fingers and toes are very cold. Ada is pale. She cannot start the car, cannot drive another inch. All of the traffic seems aimed at her. Don't start the car, Ada, we tell her. Rest. Wait. The traffic is heavy now, and if you're unsure, it's best to take no chances. Ada unfastens her seat belt and sits there, exhausted.

It is six-thirty in the evening and the highway is full of cars.

Now a word about the drivers. They turn to look as they pass, making querying hand movements. Most of them do not stop. Each car that passes rocks Ada's car with Ada inside it like a little tornado or earthquake. Ada does not want them to stop. It's all right, she signals with her hand, keep going. The cars speed by, going much too fast, *fffasst, fffasst, ffast-ffast, fffasst.*

It is six-thirty and many drivers are returning home. The cars keep racing by *ffasst-ffast,* non-stop. The sun is setting quickly. To the rear, the fruit trees of the monastery at Latrun are golden in the light, row after row of neatly planted trees, each a curly bronze whorl. A low fence runs on into the distance along the right-hand side of the road, like a very clear sentence, in the last light.

Ada reaches into the backseat for her pocketbook and places it on her knees. One after another, a handkerchief, a tissue, and a little bottle of cologne pass through her hands. Also in the back is a thick folder of scientific publications. Ada does not know when she will be able to edit them. She daubs cologne on her forehead, but the usual refreshing feeling is missing. Ada steps shakily onto the shoulder and walks back along the fence side of the car, which she leans on for support. She opens the trunk and pulls out a jerrycan, intending to splash some water on her face and hands. In the end, however, she pours the entire contents of the can on her head and all over herself, as if taking a lukewarm shower. At first she does this without meaning to; then, with a growing sense of relief. Rivulets of water run down her hair, coiling it into ringlets, and onto the shoulders of her dress.

Ada feels better. She replaces the jerrycan, slams the trunk shut, walks back to the front of the car, and leans against the right side of the hood, her white dress dripping water. She still cannot drive. A puddle collects on the pavement around her feet, all reddish gold in the sunset, like an odd celebration, a celebration of the end. Ada stands there: propping herself up, exhausted, golden. The sun has become less definite and her panic is not so acute. We can worry less about her. It is the end of sunset in the Latrun valley, in a soft and rather aloof landscape that does not detain the traveler. A white car stands parked on the right side of the road — between the car and the fence, a middle-aged woman dripping water, the shoulders of her dress turning gray and clinging damply to her body. She is resting. We are waiting.

*I*do sits by the driver of the very dusty jeep, which stops
near the Latrun junction. The driver is shod in sandals
consisting of soles and a single strap and is dirty with engine oil. The driver and Ido are silent, two people who
have spent so much time together that they have said all
there is to say and are now simply fellow travelers. Ido's
sandals are caked with dust. One of the straps is hanging
by a thread, about to tear. Ido is returning from guiding
a desert jeep tour in Sinai. His face is unshaven. By his
side are an almost empty knapsack and a rifle.

Ido is named after Ada, because Ido's mother is Ada's
best friend. Ido's mother is a woman of many commit-
tees and commissions who changes hairdos every week.
Ido's mother is the only person with whom Ada can
really laugh out loud, the way you can laugh with someone who has known you since childhood. Ada and Ido's
mother do not need many words when they talk. And
that is all we will say about Ido's mother, because she is
not on the road with us and does not belong to our story.

What does belong to our story is the fact that when
Ido was a baby, Ada, in the days before she was married
herself, was often his babysitter. She held him in her arms
and taught him such first words as *light, hot,* and *water.*
Ido, an alert and quiet infant, looked now at the ceiling
from which hung the bulb that Ada's finger switched on
and off; now at the steam from the kettle; now at his own
chubby brown hand that Ada held beneath the faucet;
and now, concentratedly, at her mouth, trying to follow
her lips which said: "water." Ada liked teaching babies
their first words, and Ido has liked Ada ever since, because she has known just how to be with him, whatever
age he is. When Ido, thin and excited, celebrated his bar
mitzvah, Ada did not dream of kissing him, but Ido

stood on tiptoe and planted a kiss on her cheek before
fleeing from his amazed family. Then he grew up and
went into the army. Although now that he is discharged
he no longer lives with his parents, he and Ada always
enjoy their rare meetings. Ada is not sentimental and
feels no need to play the tribal mother. The hopelessly
disarming encumbrance of childhood has long ceased to
come between them and they can talk. Ido likes Ada,
more than he likes her husband, Shmaryahu, who always
has a driven look. Shmaryahu's blue eyes seem frozen to
him, focused on some other world. Ido and Ada's daughters were never friendly.

Is Shmaryahu with us on the road too?

Perhaps.

*I*do gets out of the jeep, slings his knapsack and rifle over
his shoulder, and raises his hand idly: good-bye. The
driver of the jeep swings around at the intersection to
head back toward the southwest. He takes out a pair of
sunglasses and puts them on. Ido, on the other hand,
who is now walking eastward, takes off his dust goggles.
We are delighted that he is walking eastward.

Ido crosses the intersection and keeps walking
straight ahead in the direction of the mountains. His pace
is neither quick nor slow, and he enjoys stretching his
legs after several days of driving. The after-sunset light
illuminates him from behind in dull bronze tones. The
light falling on the roadside is no longer strong; a first
pallor rises from the fields. Ido halts to look for something in his knapsack. He is thin and not especially tall
and is wearing a polo shirt that is too small for him and
stained with diesel oil in the midriff from an emergency

repair in the desert. His shorts are ragged and very short. Ido is a little hungry, but not terribly. He finds a slightly discolored apple at the bottom of his knapsack and takes a bite of it. Actually, he has plenty of time. After the torrid heat of Sinai, the air is pleasant. Ido walks slowly along the roadside by the low ongoing fence. Ido likes to feel his body, the muscles of his legs.

Ada is still leaning against her car. The drivers slow down and ask her if she needs help, and she continues to wave them on gaily. Ada decides that if she still can't drive by nightfall, she'll hitch a ride to Jerusalem. Meanwhile, she'll wait to see what happens. She isn't in a hurry. There's nothing wrong with standing by the roadside. Actually, she feels all right except for having to drive. The cars speed by, *ffassst-ffasst, fffast.*

Ido, who has spied the parked car from afar, decides to walk to it. It stands to reason, he thinks, that if its driver has a problem, he may be able to fix it and catch an easy ride to Jerusalem. He tosses the rest of his apple into the oleander bushes by the roadside and continues walking eastward. The passing cars fan him with warm air.

Ido suddenly realizes that the car is Ada's and covers the remaining distance quickly. He puts an arm around her. Ido chatters gaily as a sparrow. He and Ada stand together on the side of the road; Ido talks and Ada simply smiles. A big red automobile whizzes by and screeches to a stop on the shoulder ahead of them. In it is a couple Ada knows.

They turn to look back, swiveling their heads as far as they can, and smiling broadly, ludicrously, as a communication of vigorous friendship. The man gestures with his hands. The woman rolls down her window and sticks out a disembodied head. She has on too much lipstick.

The disembodied head calls out: "Ada! Need any help?"

"No, no," answers Ada, anxious to be rid of them. She already has Ido, smile and all.

"We've got a performance in Jerusalem," shouts the woman's head apologetically, and the red automobile sets out again. We'll get along without it. Ada and Ido smile at each other.

*I*do says: "So what happened, Ada?"

"I don't know what happened. I just can't drive."

"Are you sick?"

"I don't think so. The road just frightened me all of a sudden, so I stopped."

"Want me to drive?"

"I'd appreciate it."

Ido does not hurry. Every movement is deliberate. He circles the car to its other side, moving easily, and opens the door. Ido puts his rifle in the backseat, on top of Ada's folder of manuscripts, lays his knapsack next to it, sits down behind the wheel, and stretches his legs. He leans forward to open Ada's door and says: "I've been driving nothing but jeeps for a week. What a treat your car is."

Ada sits down beside him and shudders slightly. The sun already has set, and the drop in light and temperature makes her shiver. She feels sad that the light has gone; she thinks of darkness as one of those bad times that only being old enough can get you through, with a measure of resignation. Ido has not started the car yet. He asks if she is cold. Ada is not certain. Ido asks why all that water. She tells him about the jerrycan. Ido takes off his shirt with its streak of diesel oil and begins wiping her slowly, thoroughly: first her head, then her face, then her arms, then — still unhesitatingly, though perhaps a bit too forcefully — her back and chest. Ada breathes slowly, quietly, relaxing under his hands. Ido tosses the wet shirt into the backseat. The once neatly empty seat now looks a mess with the folder, the grimy knapsack, the rifle, the discarded shirt. But Ido sits erect, a compactly built young man. His skin is tanned and dry. His vertebrae stick out like a long, stiff string of beads.

"I thought I'd dry out more quickly in this heat," says Ada with her eyes closed.

"It's because of your long hair. My mother would never go pouring jerrycans of water on herself. Her hairdo has to last all week. Have you seen the Eiffel Tower she has now? — no, not a tower, it's like a beehive. More power to her. But you don't need a hairdo. You have hair."

Ido says "hair" as though saluting. Ada smiles. Her eyes are closed.

"Look, something must have happened."

"Something did. Shmaryahu and I separated three days ago," says Ada with her eyes closed. "And you," she adds, "are the first person to hear about it."

Ido whistles lightly and looks at her.

"Is it final?"

"Yes."

Ido asks Ada if she feels good about it. Ada says that it was she who wanted it.

Ido asks: "How many years has it been? Twenty-two?"

"Twenty-three."

"Does my mother know?"

"Not yet. I told you, right now you're the only one."

Ido feels suddenly awkward. It's all a little too much for him, too much for his years. He says: "Well, talking won't get us to Jerusalem."

Ido puts the key in the ignition, turns it, and starts the car, which takes to the road, gliding forward gaily in the long line of traffic. It seems content to be its old self again. Ada looks straight ahead through half-shut lids. The air is growing gray. All colors are fading, even those of the cars on the road. We are aware of shapes now, rather than colors, moving shapes, blurry at the edges, in a lightless halo of haze like thin dust in the air, as though a curtain were covering and blotting out the earth. The fields darken quickly.

A recent flashback: three days before all this, Ada, perfectly calmly, says to Shmaryahu, who is preparing for another trip abroad, that she would rather he did not return from there to their apartment. We are sorry to hear this, but Ada is neither sorry nor surprised. She expected it. For several years now she has noticed that when setting the table, she forgets Shmaryahu's knife and fork, or sometimes his glass. That she goes to sleep and gets up in the morning looking straight ahead, as if there were no one else in the bed with her. That she immediately heads for another room to get dressed, and so does he. That their nightly battles over the blanket have been settled long ago by separate blankets. That Shmaryahu's frequent trips, his returns, the turn of his key in the door, his heavy tread with two suitcases and an overcoat over his arm—all have ceased to sound any depths and have become a mere nuisance. There goes Shmaryahu again to bring the Jews of the world to Israel, and here comes Shmaryahu again, still without the Jews of the world. Maybe next time. Ada can no longer bear the awfulness of hope. When she tells him she would rather he didn't come back, there is no violence in what she says, but the contrary: now life will be easier. Shmaryahu does not argue. I'll phone you from New York, he says, from the hotel. We'll talk it over. He takes his two suitcases and leaves, only his jaw a little slacker than usual, as if he were chewing on something.

Ada and Shmaryahu have no children left at home. Their older daughter is married, and their younger daughter is studying in Beersheba. We are concerned about them. You will have to tell them, Ada, we say: How will you do it? How will they take the news? So far, Ada has no answers. Meanwhile, she has not told anyone. Shmaryahu has not called from New York either. Perhaps he is calling now and the phone is ringing and ringing in their empty apartment. Let it ring. Now she has told Ido, who is driving her car and feeling both awkward and glad. He never much cared for Shmaryahu. He never shared his parents' sentimental opinion of the man. Ido drives, his eyes on the road, very much in charge. He is thinking that all these years it was he, not his parents, who had it right: Ada was never happy with her eminence of a husband. So who saw it all along, eh?

Ido would gladly get Shmaryahu off the road and out of this part of the story.

It's Ada and Ido, unmistakably in one car. Ido says, "We'll get there before night."

And yet he switches on the headlights. In the hazy twilight, between day and night, the cars are phantasmagorical. Ido is in need of a clearer definition of light.

Ido is an excellent driver who misses nothing. The lanes of cars surge on like a herd of heavy gray horses; now the left lane moves ahead, now the right. Now the traffic bunches up even more: something is holding it up, perhaps a tractor or a stuck car. Ada cannot bear the tension of the cars coming toward her in their passing lane, *fffasst,* as jauntily as if they owned the world; every car-shape seems about to crash into her, more out of thoughtlessness than spite. She does not know how Ido can drive without thinking of such things. Once more the traffic breaks free and flows faster. The orchards are hard to make out in the no-light.

*T*he massed mountains are in front of them now. Look, over there on the left are the lights of the gas station at Sha'ar Ha'gai where the climb begins. And over there on the right, in the dusk beneath the ruined Turkish khan, is the old beauhinia tree, heavy with hanging pods. Ido steers the car into the steep ravine through which the highway to Jerusalem runs, stretching in his seat; he can already smell the scents of the city, of wind, mountain, and many pine trees, of air that you can drink in large gulps. The change is total: coming from the desert, he is keenly aware of the difference. Hills rise on either side of them; the one on the left is closer to the road, the one on the right, farther off. Along its flank runs the road from Beth-Shemesh, which feeds into the highway and joins it.

The highway heads into the night. The air is truer now. Soon the shapes of the cars will be swallowed up and converted to many quickly moving lights in the deep earnestness couched between the mountains. Up above stand in a row the lights of a village, like fishing boats that have set sail on an ocean of darkness. Soon the cars will thin out; each car rampaging up or down the ravine will be noisy and violent, the sound reverberating into the distance while the ravine waits to calm down again. Night will close over the road, a high, stern night whose moon has set long ago. Pine trees will turn black and rustle slowly, part of the nocturnal essence. Only in the first light of dawn will they reappear by a road swabbed bright with phantom water, as fresh as on Creation's first day, with bicycles and partridges. The pines will yawn and awake to their own green. And then with much noise, will come the slow trucks shifting gears. And again, the racing cars.

*K*eeping his eyes on the road, Ido asks Ada what it's like to be separated for three whole days.

Ada says she doesn't know. Ido cannot quite believe that. But we can. Ada tells Ido's unbelieving shoulder that she really has no idea. Ido does not understand how you can have no idea about something so important. Ada says that she wishes she felt something, anything, sorrow or anger or relief, but that she doesn't feel a thing. Except for this sudden fear of the road. She is sure to get over it in a day or two. It will pass. It has to.

"What have you done these past three days?"

"Nothing special. Read manuscripts, made notes. This morning I returned a batch to the publisher in Tel

Aviv and took a new batch. I shopped for groceries. I spoke on the telephone. What does anyone do?"

Ido says with a smile that he's happy to see that Ada is wearing her white dress with the gold belt. He remembers her wearing it to his bar mitzvah. Ada can't believe he remembers.

"And how I do!" says Ido, embarrassed to glance at her. In fact, he tells her, that whole year, and all the years before and after his bar mitzvah, he was crazy about her. And scared to death that his mother would find out. Or that Ada would. He says this without daring to look at her. His imagination is already at work while he expertly pilots the wet-haired woman in distress sitting next to him with her eyes shut. Ido tries keeping his mind on the road. That's where it belongs.

Ada is happy. She moves a little nearer to him. When she opens her still half-shut eyes, she sees the thin brown body very close to her, sun-bronzed legs almost black, calm hands resting on the steering wheel. Be careful, Ada, be careful. But she has no other field of vision at the moment. Ada wants Ido now, hard; perhaps she has wanted him from the moment he appeared twenty kilometers ago. Ido casts a quick glance at her. Cunningly he reaches out as though to check if her car door is locked. But Ada's body is there to meet him. It's not your imagination, Ido.

"Why don't you rest that wet head of yours on me, you'll feel better. And if you stick your hand in my knapsack, there's one more apple there."

Ada pulls from the knapsack a pair of torn underpants, a dry soap container, a map fitted to a plastic folder, a crushed matchbox, and a bruised apple. She carelessly wipes the apple on her white dress, and Ido is pleased with her. Ada and Ido take turns taking bites from the apple. Her hair dampens his neck and shoulder and excites him a bit, making him bite his bottom lip. Their bodies were never strangers to each other. As a child he clung to her no end. And yet. The hunger is now very clear.

Ido suddenly realizes that all this will vanish into thin air once they reach Jerusalem and decides to plunge ahead.

"Listen. I'm going to pull over soon and we'll walk to the top of that hill."

"Here?" wonders Ada. It has never occurred to her before to stop her car on the highway to Jerusalem in order to go mountain climbing.

"Not right here, a little farther on. There's a real nice saddle up above us." Ido is afraid that Ada will say no, but Ada does not say anything.

Ido, responsibly, says gruffly:

"Just don't fall in love with me, because I have a girl-friend. You've met her. Her name's Ilana."

What an idiotic thing that was to say, Ido. Ada stiffens for a moment, then reflects that actually it makes things easier: all at once everything is less important, because Ido is less important too. Fine, so there's Ilana. So what. She remembers Ilana from one of those Saturday coffee klatsches at Ido's parents' house: a boyish haircut, an Arab dress from the souk, and an unpleasant voice.

Ido pulls off the road and cuts the engine. They stop. Seat belts. Windows. Doors. Air.

The car stands parked on the shoulder once more. It hasn't gone very far and here it is again.

The evening air is warm and dark, suffused with the smell of gasoline. Once more the vehicles speed by, *fffasst, ffasst, ffasst-ffast, fffasst,* rocking the car with each gust. Ido remembers to take the triangular reflector and stand it behind the parked car, so that for a moment it seems to Ada that they've just stopped for some repair. Ada regards the reflector as though it were a tombstone for something not yet identified. Reality seems to have broken up into little particles that she can't fit together again. The cars flash by with people hurrying home to their dinners and well-lit rooms. On her right, close enough to reach out and touch it, is a rocky trail. From a car you can't reach out and touch anything. Ada has her doubts about the mountain. But it's only Ido, after all.

"Up we go," says Ido, urging her on like a tour guide.

Ada climbs slowly up the mountain, which exudes the hot day's smells of pine trees and thyme and gasoline fumes and much dust. Even the insects on the pine roots are caked with dust. Ido takes big strides from rock to rock, as sure-footed as on a city sidewalk, skipping quickly and erectly with his rifle over his shoulder. Ada has to grab at something now and then to keep from slipping. She is embarrassed to be out of breath and to have to keep stopping to get her wind. It is not really a hard climb.

"Come on," Ido encourages her with a smile. "Come on, Ada, we're almost there." Here, on the mountain, he has no peer. A king.

Ada is afraid with a whole confused ocean of fears. Midway in life, as at its outset, you do not trust your body not to fail or disappoint you. Ada is glad that it is getting dark quickly. Ido seems to know the place well (Ilana?): a very bent pine tree spreads its low branches above a rockface flat as a table, a warm rock covered with pine dust and pine needles. The front of the rock drops off sharply, and Ada warns herself not to slip, because you can tumble from here all the way back down to the road.

Ada and Ido on a rockface, beneath a spreading pine tree, on top of a not very high hill. The abandoned car is almost exactly beneath them, its triangular reflector shining behind it, every detail of it familiar: the upholstery, the dashboard, the broken ashtray that hasn't been fixed for years. Everything in the car is familiar. The noise of the big highway echoes louder up here, deafeningly. But it's only Ido, after all.

"It's kind of funny to be carrying something like that around since your bar mitzvah," says Ada, as though looking for an opening.

"Better late than never."

That too, of course, is not the right phrase; but Ido's face close to hers is flaming now, his dark eyes are very earnest, and words in themselves have no value. Ada is thrilled by his new face. She could have lived her whole life and never seen it. We say: of all Ido's faces, Ada, this is the one you will remember. Ido puts down his rifle within reach and turns to her. But this is so sudden, Ada thinks. Ada drops to her knees and he quickly kneels by her side. The rock feels warm beneath her back. High up above his shoulder the sky looks unkempt: the terrible, ravaging sorrow of a night in the mountains, as though all of life existed only on a very thin, narrow strip, a flimsy bridge that alone was habitable; take a single wrong or careless step and you were banished to dead dirt where no man lived. Down below, the cars speed on and on, bringing their passengers home, a long, narrow swath with nothing beyond it. Ido's face, a long, sharp jawline in need of a shave, the tense look of a man in danger. There is a possible wound in this, Ada thinks. And an innocence.

Something in her gives now, bursts hotly, like pity. She hugs him hard; and indeed, all that is left for her to do is to step into that great sea she knows so well and let herself be taken by a wave and yet another until she picks out the biggest wave of all and rides it, breaking, back to shore; but the big wave eludes her this time, as if some dreadful, all-leveling sorrow has reduced all things; and she becomes Ido's silent witness, with no regrets.

*I*do checks and rechecks his rifle, which has pine dust in its barrel, blowing in it over and over. Ada gathers her almost dry hair and shakes dust and pine needles from her dress.

"I was too excited," he says apologetically.

"So was I, Ido." Ada's voice is very low. She is still full of an endless tenderness that fills her completely. So much Ido. And that new face.

Ido does not know what to say. He touches her forehead, her mouth, bashfully. Suddenly he jumps to his feet.

"Damn, I see some police down there by the car. I better get down and calm them before those mothers break into it and you've got a problem."

Now Ada too sees the fierce blinking blue light down below on the roadside, as if sniffing her car. We say: they won't break in so quickly, Ido, but we know that you want to get away from here. That it's all so terribly sad.

"Go on down. I'll follow you."

Ido plunges quickly downhill in leaps and bounds, as if nothing can knock him off his stride. There is a note of finality in his descent. I've lost him, thinks Ada. From now on there will always be a great self-consciousness between us, as between people who have gone too far. When I'm invited to his wedding with that Ilana of his, or with some other Ilana, there will be a problem. I've lost Ido, Ada thinks. Tomorrow I'll visit his parents, and when I take off my sunglasses, he'll count my wrinkles with open curiosity. And the day after that, with a triumphant show of sorrow, he'll take note of my first gray hairs.

Ada, in her fears, does not understand Ido, who has just persuaded two policemen in a slightly hoarse voice that everything is all right. Writing off their suspicions, they return to their vehicle and drive off with a slam of its doors. Quickly it merges with a long line of traffic that slows down for it, the fierce light winking on its roof, tinting the mountainside with a moving blue stain. Ido is now a dark shape against the car, waiting for her to come down. He is rather mortified. He thinks he has lost Ada forever, because he had his chance and disappointed like a baby. Ido is angry with himself; he stands there, full of dark fury. The sandal that was about to tear has torn. Ido removes it and goes on standing with one shoe on and one shoe off. He braces his bare foot against the side of the car, which is still giving off heat. Bad. Ido waits, angry with himself.

*T*he breeze arrives at last. At first they hear it dragging at the dry thistles with a sharp rustle, then whipping the pine boughs, which take a long, a very deep breath. Ada stretches herself: she can feel the strength run back into her wide-awake body, every bone of which feels aired by the wind. Ada looks down and knows that never again will she see the road from this angle; from now on she will drive without stopping, without looking up from the thin life-strip of the ravine. She will keep to the straight and narrow. Ada lightly touches a pine tree, al-most in farewell. But now she can drive, and that is what she decides to do. She needs only to get to the bottom, not quickly like Ido, not by leaps and bounds, but to get there. And to tell him to sit next to her while she starts the car and drives the last few kilometers to the city that broods quietly over its mountains, one more car to have arrived among the houses and the flowerbeds and the traffic lights. And to open her seat belt, and let Ido off by his house, and say the inevitably awkward good-bye, because the two of them, really, what an idea. And then home to a house that Shmaryahu would never come back to, to be by herself, and begin at last, three days late, the job of tallying and mourning.

Translated by Hillel Halkin

About the Author

© Prisma, Jerusalem

Shulamith Hareven grew up in Jerusalem, where she lives today. She has published thirteen books in Hebrew, including poetry, novels, stories, essays, a children's book in verse, and a thriller (in pseudonym). But stories remain for her the crux of all writing: "Having written in almost all genres," she explains, "I always come back to the short story or novella as a favorite, demanding form. This is where the craft of writing counts most: one cannot hide behind lengthy descriptions or convoluted plots or exotic characters or an excess of psychology. In a good short story, every word matters: change one, and the story becomes something else. That is a challenge writers love."

Though she speaks several languages, Hareven writes only in Hebrew, "the richest and most precise of 155 languages." She has served as writer-in-residence at the Hebrew University in Jerusalem and was the first (and for twelve years the only) woman member of the Academy of the Hebrew Language.

As a teenager, Hareven participated in the Hagana underground. She was a combat medic in the siege of Jerusalem in the War of Independence, an officer in Operations in the Israeli Defense Forces, and reported from the front line in the War of Attrition and the Yom Kippur War. With the help of Palestinian friends, she spent time in Arab refugee camps at the height of the Intifada, writing eyewitness reports. Her widely read press column strongly advocates the Peace Camp position in Israel. She is married and has two children and one grandchild.

Hareven draws a distinct line between her public activities and her literary work. She wishes her fiction to be judged for its literary merit and not for topical allusions. Her work has been translated into ten languages; her story "Loneliness" was chosen to represent Israel in an anthology of international women's writing. *Twilight and Other Stories* is her fourth book in English. The others are *City of Many Days, The Miracle Hater,* and *Prophet.*